BOOKS BY ROBERT NEWMAN

The Boy Who Could Fly
The Japanese
Merlin's Mistake
The Testing of Tertius
The Shattered Stone
Night Spell
The Case of the Baker Street Irregular
The Case of the Vanishing Corpse
The Case of the Somerville Secret
The Case of the Threatened King
The Case of the Etruscan Treasure
The Case of the Frightened Friend

The Case of the Frightened Friend

The Case of the Frightened Friend

by Robert Newman

Atheneum 1984 New York

LIBRARY OF CONGRESS CATALOGING IN PUBLICATION DATA

Newman, Robert
The case of the frightened friend.

SUMMARY: Andrew and Inspector Wyatt help a friend whose father has mysteriously died, whose grandfather is a complete invalid, and who has reason to suspect others in the family of wrongdoing.
[1. Mystery and detective stories] I. Title.
PZ7.N4857Casd 1984 [Fic] 83-15887
ISBN 0-689-31018-8

Published simultaneously in Canada by
McClelland & Stewart, Ltd.
Composition by Maryland Linotype, Baltimore, Maryland
Printed and bound by Fairfield Graphics,
Fairfield, Pennsylvania
Designed by Mary Ahern
First Printing December 1983
Second Printing November 1984

For Dr. Albert Martins who put the rivet in Grandfather's neck—with awe and gratitude—and for Annie, Grover and, of course, Brewster with gratitude and love.

Contents

The Case of the Frightened Friend

1

The Appeal

The four-wheeler drew up in front of a house that was very like all the other houses on the square except that it seemed to have fewer lights showing. It must have been the right one, however, for Cortland was opening the cab door. He had been even quieter than usual during the ride from Paddington, but now—abruptly and a little awkwardly—he said, "While you're here in London, will you be seeing that Scotland Yard inspector you and Chadwick were talking about?"

"Why, yes," said Andrew, somewhat surprised. "As you probably gathered, he's a friend. Why do you ask?"

"No reason," said Cortland, getting out. The cabby handed him his bag. "Thank you for the ride."

"Not at all," said Andrew. "See you back at school."

"Yes," said Cortland. He started to close the door, then pulled it open again. "If I don't come back at the end of the holiday," he said, leaning into the cab and speaking very quietly, "will you look into it?"

"What?" asked Andrew. "What do you mean?"

But, slamming the door, Cortland turned and started up the steps of the dark, quiet house, and the cab driver shook the reins and set the horse clip-clopping up the street toward Park Road and St. John's Wood.

Odd? Yes, it was, but no odder than everything else that had happened that day. The strangeness began early in the afternoon when the local doctor decided that the two boys from Andrew's house who were in the infirmary had measles. He reported this to the headmaster, and since the spring vacation was to start in three days, the head decided to send all the other boys in the house home early rather than quarantine them. Delighted at this turn of events, they were taken to the railroad station and, at the last possible moment when the train was already in sight, one of the masters arrived with Cortland, whose full name was Benedict Cortland, III. He was not in Andrew's or Chadwick's house but, the master explained, the school had just received a telegram informing them of a serious illness in Cortland's family and requesting that he be sent home immediately. Since he was a bit younger than Andrew and Chadwick, the master asked them if they'd keep an eye on him, and they said they'd be glad to and invited him into their compartment.

Cortland was quiet during the ride down to London, which didn't surprise Andrew. He didn't know Cortland well, but he'd run into him a few times walking in the hills above the school, something that Andrew liked to do and apparently Cortland enjoyed also. He had found him very quiet then, during their walks, but also very knowledgeable about any birds they saw or wildflowers they came across, and Andrew liked him.

Chadwick, however, was not quiet; and after some general conversation he began talking about something that Andrew had always found a little embarrassing; Andrew's friendship with Inspector Wyatt of Scotland Yard, whom Chadwick had once met and about whom he never tired of talking. Andrew was finally able to get him off that particular subject and on to something more neutral, and the rest of the trip passed quite pleasantly.

Chadwick, Andrew knew, lived in Belgravia, which was nowhere near where he was going. But when he discovered that Cortland lived on Sherburne Square, which was on his way home, he offered to drop him. Cortland accepted his offer gratefully, and this led to his very startling requests, one that Andrew could not decide whether he should or should not take seriously.

He was still thinking about it when the four-wheeler turned into the driveway of the house on Rysdale Road and drew up under the porte-cochere. Matson had either been waiting or, with a good butler's sixth sense, had known when Andrew would be arriving, for the cab had barely stopped before he opened the door of the house and came out.

"Welcome home, Master Andrew," he said, taking his bag.

"Thank you, Matson. I gather you knew I was coming."

"Your telegram arrived late this afternoon. Fred gave it to your mother when he called for her at the theatre."

"Is she home?"

"She's in the drawing room. And so is Miss Sara."

"Oh, good."

He paid the cab driver and went into the house. Verna must have been waiting too, for Matson had not yet closed the door behind them when she came hurrying out of the drawing room.

"Hello, Mother."

She embraced him and, unlike most of the boys at school who acted as if they would rather be boiled in oil than have any female—especially a mother or a sister—show them any sign of affection, Andrew didn't mind at all. There was good reason for this, of course. Verna's feelings for him and his for her were not only deep and genuine, but they were always displayed with discretion.

His behavior toward Sara, however, who was closer to his own age and who had followed Verna out into the entrance hall, was necessarily different.

"Good evening, Miss Wiggins," he said with exaggerated formality, noticing that she was wearing a new dress and looking very pretty.

"Good evening, Andrew," she said, following his lead and dipping in a deep curtsey, then ruining the effect by grinning impishly at him.

"I promised Sara I wouldn't comment on how much you've grown—though of course you have," said Verna. "Or how well or tired you looked after your train trip down. But, late as it is, she did give me permission to ask whether you'd had dinner."

"No, I haven't. They gave us a kind of scrappy tea before we caught the train, but—"

"Say no more," said Verna. Then, as Mrs. Wiggins came bustling in, "Well, you were right, Mrs. Wiggins."

"Of course I was," she said, hugging Andrew. Since she had known him even before she became the Tillett's housekeeper, she was not at all self-conscious about showing her affection for him. "I *am* glad to see you. Now if you'll come into the breakfast room, I had cook fix a little something for you."

The little something turned out to be everything that Andrew had hoped it might be, including cold beef and ending with his favorite apple tart. And though he had to stop several times to say hello to Annie, the downstairs maid, and Fred, the coachman, he did well enough to satisfy even Mrs. Simmonds, the cook, who took any food that was not finished as a personal affront.

"All right," said Andrew when Annie had cleared the table. "Now tell me what's been going on down here."

"No. You tell us why you're down from school so early," said Verna. "Fred insists that you were sent down for something nefarious like setting up a horse-racing pool."

"He would think that. Didn't the school's telegram say?"

"No. It just said that, due to unforeseen circumstances, you'd be coming home tonight instead of on Friday."

"Oh. Well, it was measles."

"Measles?"

He explained, trying hard to show the proper amount of sympathy for the two boys in the infirmary and at least a sign of regret for the missed days at school.

"That is too bad," said Verna, repressing a smile.

"Yes, is it. How's the play going?"

The play was an adaptation of *Jane Eyre* that Verna had done in New York to great acclaim and, because it had been such a success there, was doing again here in London.

"Oh, fine," said Verna, exchanging a quick look with Sara. "We finally got a theatre—the Windsor on the Strand—and we just started rehearsals yesterday."

"What else?"

"What do you mean?"

"There *is* something else—something you're not telling

me." Then, when neither of them said anything, "How's Peter? Have you seen him?"

"Yes, late this afternoon," said Sara. "He stopped by the theatre just as we were about to leave, and we told him you were coming home unexpectedly, and he said, if you wanted to, you could come to the Yard tomorrow and he'd take you out to lunch."

"Good-o! I was hoping I'd be able to see him and . . . Wait a minute. What were you doing at the theatre, Sara?"

Again Verna and Sara exchanged glances.

"You're going to have to tell him sometime," said Verna. "It might as well be now."

"I suppose so," said Sara. "I was there because I may be in it. The play, I mean."

"In it?"

"Yes. Playing Adele, Rochester's ward. I was dying to play the part when we were in New York, and your mother said no. That she didn't think my mum would like it. But I asked again when I heard that they were going to do the play here, and my mum said it would be all right if I kept on with school too; and your mother said she'd leave it to the director, and he liked me, so—"

"But that's wonderful!" said Andrew. "Why did you hesitate about telling me?"

But he knew. She was afraid that he'd be hurt or angry that she was going to be busy and wouldn't be able to spend time with him during the holiday as she usually did.

"Well—" she began.

"You think I haven't got things to do by myself? There are dozens of things I can do, want to do and expect to do—starting with having lunch tomorrow with Peter Wyatt!"

2

Scotland Yard

Because he was concerned—or at the very least puzzled—by what Cortland had said to him, Andrew would probably have done what he did sometime during his stay in London. But since it was more or less on his way to Scotland Yard, he did it the next morning.

Leaving a bit early, he walked over to Wellington Road, continued on along Park Road and went west to the small and dignified square where he had dropped Cortland the night before. Like most of its neighbors, the house was of dark red brick with a railed off area way in front of it and an iron gate under the bridge of the front stairs for tradesmen. He went up the steps and tugged at the polished brass bell-pull. He heard it ring, but he had to wait several minutes before the door was opened by a rather unusual butler. For though his tail-coat and striped waistcoat fit him quite well, with his crooked nose, heavy shoulders and deep chest, he looked more like a member of the fancy—an ex-pugilist—than a colleague of Matson's.

"Yes?" he said in a voice that was, to say the least, unaccommodating.

"My name's Tillett," said Andrew. "I'd like to see Benedict Cortland, Third."

"Not here," said the butler.

"I beg your pardon?"

"I said he's not here. He's at school."

"But he's not," said Andrew as the butler started to close the door. "I came down with him last night, and—"

"Who is it, Hodge?" asked a female voice.

"Someone for Master Benedict."

"Oh." A rather attractive woman appeared. She was in her early thirties, blue-eyed and wore her blonde hair wound around her head in a coronet braid. "You're a friend of Benedict's?"

"Yes. My name's Tillett, and I came down from school with him yesterday. As a matter of fact, I dropped him off here on my way home. But your butler said—"

"I heard what he said. What he meant is that Benedict is out at the moment. Your name's Tillett?"

"Yes."

"I'm Benedict's stepmother." She spoke with a slight accent that Andrew could not identify. "If you're a friend—and I'm sure you are—Benedict will be sorry he missed you. But perhaps you can stop by again another time."

"If I may, I'd like to. Thank you, Mrs. Cortland."

"Not at all. Goodbye."

"Goodbye." And bowing, he turned and went down the steps.

As he walked over toward Baker Street where he planned to pick up an omnibus, he was even more puzzled—and more concerned—than he had been before. He was convinced that if Mrs. Cortland had not intervened, the butler would have shut the door in his face, insisting that Cortland was not there. That made it look as if they didn't want him to see Cortland, which in turn made it look as if Cortland had had good reason to be anxious and act the way he had.

He got off the bus at Westminster Bridge and walked up the Embankment to the Yard. He stood there for a moment, looking up at the steep-roofed, turreted building that was the most famous police headquarters in the world. Then he went through the gate, crossed the courtyard and gave his name to the sergeant at the desk inside, saying he wanted to see Inspector Wyatt. The sergeant gave a note to a constable, who went upstairs and came down a few moments later, nodding to the sergeant who asked Andrew if he knew where the inspector's office was. Andrew said he did, climbed two flights of stairs and knocked at the familiar door.

Wyatt, sitting at his desk in the small and crowded office, looked up when he came in.

"So what the jungle drums told me was true," he said. "Were you rusticated for bashing a master or possibly an old boy?"

"Fred thought I'd been sent down because I'd set up a horse-racing pool, but it was nothing so imaginative or heroic. It was because of measles."

"Measles?"

"Yes."

"I hope you're not contagious," he said when Andrew explained.

"I don't think I am. I didn't mention it, but I think I had measles a few years ago, and I don't think you can get it again."

"We'll pretend that's so anyway. Outside of that, how are you?"

"Fine."

The door opened, and Sergeant Tucker came in. Well over six feet tall and proportionately broad, he immediately made the office seem too small.

"Well, well," he said. " 'The school-boy with his satchel and shining morning face, creeping like a snail unwillingly to school.' "

"What's this?" Andrew asked Wyatt.

"It's known as secondary education," said Wyatt.

"I beg your pardon?"

"His daughter's studying *As You Like It* in school,

and when he helps her memorize an assignment, some of it sticks."

"Does one have to be a varsity graduate or go to an expensive public school to be able to appreciate Shakespeare?" asked Tucker with wounded dignity.

"Heaven forbid!" said Wyatt. "I think the groundlings at the Globe Theatre probably appreciated him more than a good many of the nobs in the boxes."

"Is that what I am, a groundling?"

"What you would have been. But that's enough of that. What news on the Rialto?"

"Is that Shakespeare, too?"

"*Merchant of Venice*. Well?"

"Three more last night," said Tucker, handing him a report.

"That's nice," said Wyatt dryly.

"Nice as a pennysworth of silver spoons," agreed Tucker.

"Three what?" asked Andrew.

"Never mind!" said Wyatt. "I've had enough of your getting involved in our cases." He finished reading the report. "All right," he said to Tucker. "I'll stop by again later and see if I can come up with any new ideas." Then to Andrew, "Ready for lunch?"

"If you are."

"You'll hold down the fort, Tucker?"

"Sir!" said Tucker with a heel-clicking, exaggerated salute.

They walked up Whitehall to a pub near Charing Cross where Andrew established his claim to a table while Wyatt collected sandwiches, beer and ginger beer for their lunch.

"Well," said Wyatt while they were eating, "what news on *your* Rialto?"

"Nothing very much at school besides the measles. And you probably know more about what's going on here than I do."

"The play, you mean. And the fact that Sara's going to be in it."

"Yes."

"Do you mind?"

"She seemed to be worried about that, too. Why on earth should I mind? She's mad about the theatre, would love to be an actress and was dying to play that particular part when the play was on in New York. So I think it's wonderful."

"So do I. It's like your mother to be giving her this chance. Not that she would have if she didn't think she was good. Nothing else?"

"No," said Andrew. Then, after a pause. "Well, maybe there is. Something I'd like to ask your advice about, anyway."

When Wyatt nodded, he told him about Cortland: first, the little he knew about him personally, then what he had said when Andrew had dropped him off the night before and finally what had just happened with the butler.

Wyatt sat quietly for a moment, making overlapping rings on the scrubbed wooden table with the wet bottom of his beer mug.

"I know you don't know him well, but . . . Does this seem like him? Would he be likely to say what he did to you just to be melodramatic, make himself important?

"No. It's very *un*like him. I heard from one of the chaps in his house that he's an orphan. But *he* never said so. He never talks about himself at all."

"And you, of course, wouldn't blow it all up, make a mountain out of a molehill, just to give yourself something interesting to do over the holiday, would you?"

Andrew looked at him without saying anything, and Wyatt nodded.

"All right. I apologize, but the point had to be made. And there's another one I should make. Or at least mention. If you remember your fairy tales, you'll recall that stepmothers are not very popular figures. As a matter of fact, they're usually the villain of the piece. And for reasons that go quite deep."

"I know. You think that Cortland wanted to build up a case against her?"

"I never met either of them, so I can't say. And let's remember that it was the butler who tried to keep you from seeing him, said he wasn't there, not the stepmother. What I'd suggest is that you try again to see him. If you can't, then we'll consider what can be done about it. And if you do see him, then perhaps he'll tell you why he said what he did."

"That makes sense. Thank you."

"Not at all. What are you going to do now? How are you planning to spend the rest of the afternoon."

"I've no real plans. I thought I might walk over to the theatre and say hello to Mother and Sara."

"I'd like to do that myself. I'll go with you."

They went over to the Strand and then up it to the theatre, which was almost opposite the Savoy. The theatre had been dark for some months, and there was nothing on the marquee to indicate what the last play there had been. Wyatt, who had been there before, took Andrew down the alley that led to the stage door. The pavement in front of the theatre had not been particularly clean, and the alley was even worse. Andrew stumbled over half bricks, empty bottle and pieces of wood that had probably broken off old, discarded theatre sets.

Wyatt pulled open the heavy iron door. Inside, sitting in a small booth, was a grey-haired, elderly man in a shiny dark suit. He was tall, lean and seemed to have some kind of throat complaint for when he talked his voice was hoarse and a little wheezy.

"Yes, gentlemen?" he said. "What can I do for you?"

"We've come to see Miss Tillett. This is her son, Andrew. And my name is Wyatt."

"How do you do?" said the man, bobbing his head. "Sorry I had to ask, but that's part of my job. I'll know you next time."

"You're new here, aren't you?" said Wyatt.

"Yes, sir. Just started this morning. Name of Burke. Tim Burke."

"Is my mother here?" asked Andrew.

"She is. And Mr. Harrison, the manager, and several of the others. They're out front. Best way to get to them is along here, across the stage and down."

They thanked him and went along into the wings. The backstage was lit by unshaded gas jets, whose yellow fan-shaped flames did little to relieve the darkness. They walked past a row of ropes that raised and lowered the heavy curtains and the sets that had been pulled up to the flies overhead. The footlights had not been lit, and the bare, dusty stage was illuminated by a pair of Veritas oil lamps—one on each side of the proscenium—whose circular wicks gave off almost as much light as limelights.

"Oh, Andrew," called Verna from somewhere in the shadowy auditorium. "And Peter. Come on down here."

They could not see her till they had crossed the stage and gone down the temporary steps that led to the orchestra. She was sitting just off the central aisle with Sara, Mr. Harrison and several men and women Andrew did not know.

Andrew did know Mr. Harrison, the manager, and

apparently Wyatt did, too, for they greeted one another and Verna introduced both of them to Richards, the director, and to the other members of the company who were there.

"Sara's about to read for the part of Adele," said Verna. "You can stay and hear her if you like."

"Read?" said Andrew quietly. "I thought it was all settled."

"Not quite. I thought she was very good and so did Richards, but Mr. Harrison hasn't had a chance to hear her yet, and we all thought he should."

"I see. Would you mind if we stayed?" Andrew asked Sara.

Though she was suddenly quite pale, Sara shook her head. Andrew and Wyatt sat down with the others, and Verna and Sara went up the steps on to the stage. Since Verna had been in the play in New York, she did not need a script. And while Sara had one in her hand, she apparently already knew most of the part by heart, for she almost never referred to it.

The scene they were doing was one near the opening of the play where Verna, as Jane Eyre, meets Adele, the young French girl who is Rochester's ward and whom she is to take care of. Andrew remembered how jealous Sara had been of the girl who had played the part in New York, and they had not done more than a few minutes of the scene before it was obvious to him that Sara was much better than the other girl. He didn't know where she had gotten the slight touch of French accent, but it was exactly right, and so was the mixture of enthusiasm and shyness with which she spoke, the awkwardness with which she moved. He knew then, as he had always suspected, that she was a born actress.

They finished the scene, the manager and director exchanged glances, and apparently there was no need for them to say anything to each other.

"All right, Sara, that's fine," said Richards. "Everyone on stage, and we'll start a reading from the very beginning."

"You mean I've got the part?" asked Sara uncertainly.

"Of course you have, darling," said Verna. "You were splendid."

"You were indeed," said Harrison. "We're delighted to have you with us. Are you staying?" he asked Wyatt.

"No. I only stopped by with Andrew to say hello. I'll be running along now."

"So will I," said Andrew.

He went up on to the stage with Wyatt and Harrison. Sara, flushed now instead of pale, was in such a happy daze that she was hardly aware of it when Andrew congratulated her, said goodbye to her and Verna, and told them he'd see them that evening.

He, Wyatt and Harrison went out and up the alley to the Strand. They stood there for a few minutes talking about Sara, Verna and the play, then Harrison went off up the Strand to his office, and Wyatt went the other way toward Scotland Yard.

Andrew glanced at his watch. It was a little before three. There was no need for him to go home for quite a while yet. Should he take a walk along the Embankment or perhaps over to Soho? Then he remembered what Wyatt had said about Cortland. Why not try to see him again now?

Walking back to Charing Cross, he caught a green City Atlas bus, and about a half-hour later got off again just before Regent's Park and walked over to Sherburne Square.

For the second time that day, he tugged at the bell-pull and, after a moment, the odd-looking butler, Hodge, opened the door.

"Good afternoon. Is Cortland here now?"

"I'll inquire. The name's Tillett?"

"Yes."

Almost reluctantly he admitted Andrew to the entrance hall, knocked at a closed door to the right of it, then went in, closing the door behind him.

The entrance hall was dark, the only light a fanlight over the door, but Andrew could see one door to the right, one to the left and a flight of stairs ahead of him. The door to the right opened, and Mrs. Cortland came out followed by a distinguished-looking man with greying hair and a short, square-cut beard.

"I'm very glad you stopped in again," she said. "Benedict came home shortly after you left. This is Dr. Thurlow. Andrew Tillett."

"How do you do, sir?"

"Hello," said the doctor, studying him with a pair of very sharp eyes. "You're a friend of Benedict's?"

"Yes, sir. At least, we're at school together."

"You're older than he is, aren't you?"

"A year or so. But we like many of the same things."

"What sort of things?"

"Oh, walking, birds, flowers."

The doctor continued looking at him for a moment, then he nodded.

"Why don't you get Benedict for his friend, Hodge?"

"Yes, doctor," said Hodge, and as if this was what he had been waiting for, he turned and went up the stairs.

"Won't you come into the drawing room?" asked Mrs. Cortland.

"Thank you," said Andrew, and he followed her and the doctor into a room that was rather dark, for the heavy drapes were half drawn.

"Tillett's an unusual name," said Mrs. Cortland, sitting down on a settee.

"Is it? I never thought that it was particularly."

"Where do you live?" asked the doctor with what was apparently his habitual directness.

"Rysdale Road in St. John's Wood."

"So it really was on your way when you dropped Benedict off here last night."

"Yes, it was."

"Very nice out in St. John's Wood," said the doctor. Then, as something came to him. "Tillett. Any relation to Verna Tillett?"

"She's my mother."

"Is she someone I should know?" asked Mrs. Cortland.

"She's an actress," said the doctor. "And a very good one. Isn't she doing a play soon?"

"Yes. *Jane Eyre*. She played in it in New York, and she's just started rehearsing it here."

Cortland appeared in the doorway, stood there as if waiting to be invited in.

"Come in, Benedict," said Mrs. Cortland. "Here's your friend, Andrew Tillett."

"Hello, Cortland," said Andrew.

"Hello," said Cortland, coming into the room and somehow looking even younger than he did at school; younger and more lost.

"I stopped by this morning, but you were out."

"Yes. Hodge told me that you'd been here."

"I thought, if you liked, perhaps we could do something together."

"When?"

"Well, what about tomorrow?"

Cortland looked at his stepmother who, in turn, looked at Dr. Thurlow, then smiled.

"That sounds like a very nice idea. Would you like to come for lunch, Andrew?"

Andrew hesitated a moment. If he was going to see Cortland, he wanted to see him alone.

"I'm afraid I can't make it for lunch. Why don't we make it after that, say around two o'clock?"

Again Cortland looked at his stepmother.

"That will be fine," he said. "See you then."

Andrew said goodbye to Mrs. Cortland and the doctor and went out. Hodge closed the door after him, and he went down the steps. He was glad he had followed Wyatt's suggestion, for he had seen Cortland. But he felt more decidedly than ever that something was wrong, and he hoped Cortland would tell him what it was when he next saw him.

3

Cortland's Problem

The next day was one of those early spring days that are so unexpectedly pleasant that you feel it would be a crime to spend any part of it indoors. Andrew walked to the Cortland house. This time Hodge let him in without any hesitation, called Cortland, and a few minutes after Andrew had rung the bell, they were outside and having a discussion as to what they should do. Though there was, in fact, very little discussion. For when Andrew suggested that they go to the zoo in Regent's Park, Cortland agreed immediately, and that was that.

They entered the zoo by the south entrance. The animals seemed to be enjoying the fine day as much as the humans: the lions pacing their cage and giving their muttering roar; the gibbons whooping; and the seals and sea lions splashing as they dived into their pools, chased one another, then climbed out only to dive in again.

They walked past the southern ponds, past the bustard,

crane and stork enclosure to the Great Western Aviary, where even more colorful birds like flamingoes, ibises and herons flew, stood or stalked. Because they were both interested in birds, they had gravitated toward them naturally. And even before they got to the Great Aviary, it was clear to Andrew that Cortland knew considerably more about them—especially the rarer, more exotic birds—than he did. When he said something about this, Cortland shrugged.

"I should know something about them," he said. "I've been here quite a few times with my grandfather. He's a bit of a naturalist."

"What's his name?"

"Benedict Cortland."

"Then your father's Benedict Cortland, Junior."

"He was. He's dead."

"Oh. Let's sit down." He led Cortland to a bench on the far side of the aviary. "You've been on my mind a good deal since we came down from school."

"I'm sorry."

"No need to be sorry, but I wish you'd tell me why you said what you did when I dropped you off at your house."

"I'm not sure I know why."

"Don't do that, Cortland. We don't know each other well, but I know you well enough to be sure you didn't do it for effect. That there was some reason for it. And I wish you'd tell me what it was."

Cortland took so long to answer that Andrew began to think he wasn't going to. But finally he said, "You're right. I did have my reasons. And to be honest, I think this is exactly what I hoped might happen. That you'd ask me about it. But now that you have—" He paused again, then said somewhat awkwardly, "I'm afraid I'll have to give you some background."

"Go ahead. We've got all afternoon."

"All right. My mother died about five years ago, when I was seven. My father was away at the time—he was in the navy—and that's when I got to know grandfather. He'd just got back from one of his trips. He moved into the house and stayed with me until my father came back. Shortly after that my father gave up active sea duty and became naval attaché, first at our embassy in Copenhagen and then in Berlin. About two years ago, just before he left Denmark, he married a Danish countess."

"Your stepmother?"

"Yes."

"I thought she had a slight accent, but I couldn't place it. Go on."

"Well, about six months ago—shortly after I came up to school—my father died."

"As recently as that?"

"Yes."

"Hard lines."

"Yes. I liked him—liked him a lot. We used to sail

together, swim, fish. My grandfather was away at the time—in Africa—and while my stepmother tried to do something about the way I felt, it wasn't any good. I'd only been with her during holidays and hardly knew her, and besides I had a feeling that she didn't really care about me."

Andrew nodded. He had sensed that himself.

"I'd been at school, and I went back up there after the funeral," Cortland continued. "About two months ago, when my grandfather got back, he came up to see me. He had quite a few things to say about what a good man my father had been, a fine naval officer and all that, and about how he—my grandfather—would be around for a while yet and look out for me and help take care of me. But all the while I had the feeling that there was something on his mind, something worrying and upsetting him, that he wasn't telling me about."

"Did you say anything to him about it?"

"As a matter of fact, I did. And he looked at me strangely and said I was more like my father than he'd realized and maybe he did have something on his mind. But he didn't want to talk about it—not then. He said he was going away again for a while—there was something he had to take care of—and when he came back, maybe he would tell me what it was all about."

"Has he come back?"

"Yes. Just the other day."

"And has he told you what he said he would?"

"No."

"Why not?"

"When the headmaster told me he'd gotten a telegram saying that something had happened and asking that I be sent home immediately, I sensed that something had happened to Grandfather. And I was right. When I got home, I discovered that he'd come back the day before and that he'd had a stroke. He's in his old room, just across the hall from mine, completely paralyzed and unable to move or even speak."

Andrew cleared his throat. "I don't know what to say. I don't think there's anything I can say."

"No."

"Is all this why you said what you did to me?"

"Yes. I had a feeling that after what had happened to my father and now to my grandfather—though I didn't know what it was yet—that something might very well happen to me. Because I had this feeling that something was very, very wrong. And now that I've seen Grandfather, I'm more convinced of it than ever."

"Why do you say that?"

"I don't know. It's just a feeling I have. And that's why I'd like you to come and see him."

"Your grandfather?"

"Yes."

"But why? I'm not a doctor."

"He's got a doctor. Dr. Thurlow. You met him yesterday. But I don't think that's what he needs."

"What then?"

"He needs what I talked to you about the other day: someone who'll look into the whole thing, really look into it."

"You mean the way Inspector Wyatt would?"

"Yes."

"But that's ridiculous! I'm not a detective either."

"No, but you know someone at Scotland Yard. And if you think something's wrong, you'd know what to do about it."

"I suppose I could talk to the inspector. I said something to him about you yesterday. And it's true your butler acted very strangely when I stopped by yesterday morning."

"How?"

"He said you were still at school. And when I said I'd come down with you the night before, your stepmother came out and said he meant that you weren't home at the moment."

"But I *was* home. This is the first time I've been out since I came down from school. Hodge must have had orders not to let anyone see me."

"Then why did your stepmother tell me to come back?"

"Once she knew you knew I was there, she must have realized you'd be suspicious if you couldn't see me." Then, as Andrew nodded, "*Will* you come back to the house with me, come up and see my grandfather?"

"If there *is* something wrong, will they let me see him?"

"If they won't, won't that be proof that there *is* something wrong?"

"Not necessarily. If he's had a stroke and is as ill as you say, he's probably not supposed to have visitors—certainly not someone who's not even a member of his family."

"Well, will you at least try it?" His eyes were on Andrew's face. "I told you about my father. He must have been very brave. But I'm not. I keep trying to be, but . . . Well, I can't help it. I'm frightened. I'm very frightened."

Andrew looked at him. He wasn't as sure as Cortland was that he'd be able to tell if something was wrong, but it was clear that it was very important to Cortland that he do *something*.

"All right," he said. "I'll come back with you. And, if we can manage it, I'd like to see him."

Cortland's face lit up.

"Thank you," he said. "Thank you very much."

Though ordinarily they would both have been happy to spend not just the afternoon but all day at the zoo, they left immediately and walked back to Sherburne Square the way they had come. Cortland had a key, but as he started to use it, Hodge opened the door.

"Oh, hello, Hodge. We're back a bit early. Is my mother home?"

"In the drawing room."

"How's my grandfather?"

"So far as I know, there's been no change. But when Dr. Thurlow arrives, perhaps he'll have something to say."

"Right. We're going upstairs. I want to show Tillett my butterfly collection."

"Yes, Master Benedict."

He closed the door, and Cortland led Andrew up the stairs. A hall ran from the back of the house to the front, and several doors opened off it.

"This is my room," said Cortland, pointing to one to the left near the top of the stairs. "And that's Grandfather's," he whispered, nodding to the one opposite. Glancing around, he opened it, beckoned Andrew in and closed the door after him.

They were in a good-sized, high-ceilinged room with windows overlooking the square. There was a bed, a chest and several chairs in it. And in the bed, lying as still as a statue, was a striking-looking man. He was probably in his seventies, with a high-bridged aquiline nose and dark blue eyes. His hair was silvery white, worn rather long, and his face, once apparently ruddy, now looked waxen. He was breathing slowly and with a certain amount of difficulty. And though he was clearly very ill and could not seem to move anything else, his eyes were clear and alive and—in a way Andrew could not identify—indomitable. They went to Cortland's face as soon as he came within their field of vision, went from there to Andrew's face, and remained there.

"Hello, Grandfather," said Cortland. "How are you this afternoon?"

The old man closed his eyes, then opened them again.

"This is a friend of mine from school, Andrew Tillett."

"How do you do, sir?" said Andrew. "Cortland has told me a great deal about you. I was sorry to hear about your illness."

Again the old man closed and then opened his eyes, not once but twice. His eyes remained fixed on Andrew's face, and Andrew not only sensed a keen intelligence behind them but had a sudden feeling that the old man was trying to communicate with him. On an impulse, he closed and then opened his eyes three times. Immediately the old man blinked three times. He *was* trying to communicate with him! He was!

Andrew knew about the Morse code, the system of dots and dashes that telegraphers used to send their messages. But even if Cortland's grandfather knew it, he—Andrew—didn't, so that was no good. But there must be *something* he could do.

He looked at the night table next to the old man's bed. There was a glass and carafe of water on it, some bottles of medicine and a thermometer. Behind the night table, in the wall, was a brass-rimmed opening like the mouthpiece of the speaking tube one used to call down to the kitchen. And of course, if you could speak through it, that meant you could hear through it too—hear most of what went on in the room.

It was then, when he realized that if something *was* wrong he'd have to be careful, that he thought of what he could do.

"He seems to be having trouble breathing," he said to Cortland. "I think we should raise him up a little."

Cortland looked puzzled but, gathering that Andrew had some reason for it, said, "All right."

"You take that side, and I'll take this," said Andrew, going to the side away from where the speaking tube was. Bending down as if he were about to lift the old man, he whispered in his ear, "Blink once for yes, twice for no. Can you hear me?"

The old man blinked once.

"Were you trying to send us a message?"

One blink. Yes.

"Do you need help?"

One blink. Yes.

What form should that help take? How could he phrase the question so that it could be answered with a yes or no? He'd have to take a chance on it.

"Do you want us to get you away from here?"

As the old man again blinked once for yes, there were footsteps on the stairs, and Andrew only had time enough to straighten up and step back away from the bed when the door opened and Dr. Thurlow came in, followed by Cortland's stepmother.

"What are you doing in here, Benedict?" she asked severely.

"I wanted to see how Grandfather was, and since I'd been talking about him to Tillett, I thought I'd bring him in with me to meet him."

"You should know he's not well enough for that," said the doctor reasonably. "We don't mind *your* coming in. As we told you, we think that's a very good idea. I gather your grandfather is fonder of you than he is of anyone else, and it's good for him to see you and know that you're concerned about him. But I don't think you should bring anyone else in."

"I should have known better," said Andrew. "I'm sorry."

"It wasn't your fault," said Cortland.

"Yes, it was. I think I'd better run along. Goodbye, Mrs. Cortland. Goodbye, doctor. Perhaps we can spend another afternoon together one of these days, Cortland."

"That would be very nice," said Cortland. And it was clear from his looks as well as the way he said it that he wasn't sure whether Andrew meant it or not.

"Well, what do you expect me to do about it?" asked Wyatt.

It was about an hour later, and Andrew had just finished his account of what had happened.

"I don't know. You told me to try to see Cortland

again, and I did, and it's obvious that something is wrong there—very wrong!"

"Am I supposed to take your word for that?"

"Are you saying you don't believe what I told you?"

"No. I think you're telling me the truth about what you *believe* happened. I'm just wondering if there may not be some other explanation for it."

"What, for instance?"

"I don't know. Do you want to take a walk with me while I think about it?"

"Where are you going?"

"To the Strand."

"The theatre?"

"Near there. If you want, you can go on, watch some of the rehearsal and go home with your mother and Sara."

"All right. I'll walk with you anyway."

They went out the rear entrance of the Yard, past the Foreign Office and along Whitehall to the Strand. They were about a half-block from the theatre when Sergeant Tucker came out of Bedford Street, nodded to Andrew and saluted Wyatt.

"Anything?" asked Wyatt. He sighed when Tucker shook his head. "There are days when you just can't make tuppence," he said. Then, turning to Andrew, "I'm sorry. There's something else I have to take care of right now. But I think that what you told me warrants looking into, and we'll do that tomorrow."

What does a policeman mean when he says there's something he has to take care of? Clearly Wyatt and Tucker were on a case and one that had something to do with this part of London, since they both seemed to be spending a good deal of time here.

But the Cortlands—young Cortland and his grandfather—were much more on Andrew's mind as he walked up the Strand than Wyatt's case, whatever it was. Which brought up the question of how much he should tell Sara of what had been happening.

It was something that had never arisen before. Whenever they had become involved in anything, they had both been in it and each of them knew everything the other knew. But with Sara in the play, everything was different. However, Andrew could not help feeling that there was so much to the Cortland case that he'd better let her know about it because he had a feeling that before it was all over she might have to become involved, too.

And so, sitting in the back of the darkened theatre with her while the director rehearsed one of the many scenes in which she did not appear, he did tell her. He had already mentioned Cortland to her, told her that they had come down from school together. That Cortland had seemed worried and upset and that he'd probably see him sometime during the holidays. Now he told her what had happened that afternoon and what Wyatt had said.

She was silent for several moments when he had finished. Silent for so long, in fact, that he finally asked her what she was thinking about.

"I don't know if you can call it thinking," she said. "I was wondering if I'm not a little sorry that I'm in the play. Because, if I wasn't, I'd be in this other thing with you."

"The play's much more important," he said.

"It is to me. But in other ways, this other thing could be much more important. Of course, it sounds as if you've got Peter interested in it now—and you couldn't have anyone better than that."

"What about you?" he said, smiling.

"Don't joke about it. I'm serious. But will you keep on letting me know what happens? Not only because I want to know, but because—if there's anything I can do—I'd like to do it."

"Of course I'll let you know."

"Starting with tomorrow?"

"Why tomorrow?"

"Didn't Peter say he was really going to look into the whole thing tomorrow?"

"Yes, he did. And I'll tell you everything that happens, everything we find out, if we do find out anything."

4

The Stricken Grandfather

About ten o'clock the next morning, a gleaming black brougham drawn by a handsome bay drew up before the Cortland house. The uniformed coachman jumped down from the box, opened the door and stood there holding it while a gentleman got out of the carriage. He was every bit as imposing as the brougham, which an informed observer would have recognized as one of Mulliner of Liverpool's best. He was in his middle forties, with just a touch of grey in his mustache and carefully trimmed beard. He wore a frock coat, striped trousers, and his gleaming top hat was cocked forward over his right eye. He was of little more than average height, but the way he carried himself made him seem much taller. He went up the steps and rang the bell. Hodge, who had seen Mrs. Cortland out only a few minutes before, opened the door almost immediately.

"The name's Reeves," said the man in a clipped and authoritative voice. "I understand my old friend Cortland's back in London."

"He is, sir," said Hodge. "But unfortunately, he's ill."

"Ill? Ill how?"

"He's had a stroke. Quite a severe one, I'm sorry to say, and . . ."

"What? All the more reason why I must see him!" and he pushed the door open all the way.

"I'm sorry, sir, but that's impossible."

"Impossible?" Reeves' tone made it clear who and what *he* considered impossible.

"As I said, he's quite ill. The doctor has forbidden any visitors. Mrs. Cortland, his daughter-in-law, is out at the moment, but if you came back when she is at home—"

"I don't want to see her. I want to see him. And I'm not a visitor. I'm a friend." As he spoke, he pushed past Hodge and went up the stairs. Staring after him helplessly, Hodge noted that he seemed to know exactly where to go. Opening the door of old Mr. Cortland's room, he went in and closed it behind him.

When he came downstairs about ten minutes later, Reeves' face was grave. He walked past Hodge without saying anything to him—without even looking at him—went down the steps and got into the brougham.

"Hospital," he said to the coachman, who saluted, closed the door and climbed back into the box.

"Well done," said Wyatt as the carriage started.

"Wasn't very difficult. Though I suppose it might have been if the lady had been there."

"Which is why we waited. I gather you saw him?"

"Yes."

"And?"

"There's something very odd about his condition. Thurlow's a good man—very good—but I don't think it's a stroke."

"What do you think it is?"

"I'm not sure. I have a few ideas, but I want to go over some material I have in my library before I say." He looked at Andrew who sat next to Wyatt. "Was there a nurse there when you saw him?"

"No, doctor."

"Wasn't one there now either. Which is something else that struck me as curious. Your friend never mentioned one?"

"No, doctor. I don't suppose you saw him. Young Cortland, I mean."

"A boy stuck his head out of the room opposite just as I was leaving, but I didn't say anything to him." He turned back to Wyatt. "I should like to get him to St. Mary's where I could give him a proper examination. And of course he should have much more care than he's getting now."

"I know."

"Will you be able to do anything about it?"

"I don't know. This was a first step, getting your opinion. For which I'm very grateful, by the way."

"Nonsense. Glad to do it. Never met the old gentleman myself, but my father knew him, and of course I've heard of him. Can I take you anywhere?"

"I don't think so. Andrew and I are going the other way. Drop us anywhere along here, and we'll get a hansom."

"Very well." Dr. Reeves rapped on the roof, and the carriage stopped. "I'll hear from you then?"

"I hope so," said Wyatt, getting out.

Andrew followed him, and by the time he had closed the door, Wyatt had flagged a hansom.

"Where to, sir?" asked the cabby.

"The Admiralty," said Wyatt, getting in and moving over so as to leave room for Andrew.

5

The Admiralty

"What do you know about the Admiralty?" asked Wyatt as the hansom turned off Marylebone Road into Portland Place.

"Well, I know what it does. That it's responsible for the administration of the navy," said Andrew.

"Do you think that's important?"

"Why, yes. I'd say it was quite important."

"I'd advise you not to be so tentative there, at the Admiralty. It's their contention that we couldn't exist without a navy. And they have a point. Since this is an island, we do need a navy, not only to protect us here at home, but to protect the shipping that brings us all the food and other things we need."

Andrew nodded. That was clear enough. "Who are we seeing there?" he asked.

"Do you know what the structure of the Admiralty is, how it's run?"

"I know that it's very complicated, with a board that includes a first lord and naval lords and a civil lord and I don't know what else."

"Included in the what else is the permanent secretary, who is a very important member of that very important body. The present one is Sir Arthur Barry, and that's who we're going to see."

"Just like that? I mean, can you see someone that important any time you want?"

"Certainly not. I sent him a note yesterday, and he made an appointment with me for eleven-thirty."

"That's what I wanted to know."

"Why?"

"Because, when I saw you yesterday afternoon, you claimed you weren't sure that something was wrong with Cortland's grandfather. But if you sent a note to Sir Arthur, you must have been sure that something *was* wrong even before you brought Dr. Reeves there this morning."

"Are you trying to evaluate your judgment or mine?"

"Either or both," said Andrew with a grin.

They came down the Haymarket, through Trafalgar Square, and the hansom drew up in front of the colonnade on Whitehall. Wyatt paid the cabby, and they entered the dark brick building. Wyatt gave his card to a uniformed commissionaire who sat at a large circular desk. He checked the name against an appointment list, summoned a page, who led them up a stair and along a corridor to an elaborately carved door with a large brass knob. He knocked, then opened the door.

Several clerks worked at desks set against the walls, but standing in the center of the room and waiting for them was a soberly dressed man in his late forties. He was lean and erect and reminded Andrew of an elegant and expertly furled umbrella.

"Inspector Wyatt? I'm Dixon. Sir Arthur is expecting you. Will you come this way?"

He opened another door, stood aside and let them precede him into another, larger room with a high ceiling and a handsome marble mantle. Sitting at a large mahogany desk near the windows was a sturdy, white-haired man, whose ruddy complexion and blue eyes spelled sea as clearly as if he'd been wearing a uniform rather than an old-fashioned double-breasted frock coat.

"Delighted to meet you, Inspector," he said, smiling and holding out his hand. "I've heard a great deal about you from Sir Roger and from other friends of mine."

"You're very kind, Sir Arthur," said Wyatt, bowing. "As you gathered from my note, I wanted to talk to you about Captain Benedict Cortland, Junior, and his father. Since this was so, I hoped you would not mind if I brought along a young friend of mine, Andrew Tillett, who is also a friend of Benedict Cortland, Third."

"Not at all. I know better than to question any of the mysterious things the Yard does its wonders to perform. By the same token, I think we should keep Dixon here. You've met?"

"Yes," said Wyatt.

"Good. Many people are under the illusion that I run this department. But those who really know are aware that it's run by the permanent secretary of the permanent secretary. In other words, by Dixon."

"As you've probably heard, Inspector," said Dixon in his quiet, cultivated voice, "Sir Arthur is as well known for his sense of humor as for his intelligence, his organizing ability and his diplomatic skill."

"There he goes again. Nothing I can do about the fellow. Now tell us exactly what we can do for you, Inspector."

"I'd appreciate your telling me anything you can about Captain Cortland and his father."

"I had Dixon bring me his file when I got your note. I've just been going over it, and while there are some things in it that are confidential—we're very jealous of our security here—I believe I can tell you most of what you want to know. I assume that afterwards you'll tell me why you're interested in him."

"Of course."

"To begin with," said Sir Arthur, opening a folder on his desk, "his active career in the navy was unexceptionable. He was one of the youngest captains we've ever had in the service and one of the best."

"If that's so, why did he give up his active career and become a naval attaché?"

"I am at least partly responsible for that. I knew his father slightly and admired him very much. Captain Cortland came to my attention when there was first talk of ceding Heligoland to Germany. The captain was violently opposed to this. He was, in fact, so outspoken that the Foreign Office took note of it and questions were asked about it in the House."

"When was this?"

"About three years ago. I had him come in to see me and explained that an officer in Her Majesty's Navy should not be making the kind of political statements he was making. He disagreed, saying the issue concerned not just the future of the navy but the future of Britain and, as such, was more important than his career. I could not help but admire his position. After talking further, I suggested that if he was as interested in broad policy matters as he seemed to be that he consider leaving active service and becoming a naval attaché where what he had to say would affect policy decisions. He thought about it and finally agreed with me."

"It was as a result of his talk with you, then, that he became a naval attaché."

"Yes. In Copenhagen. He did extremely well there, was highly respected at the embassy and married a Danish countess. And when there was an opening in Berlin, we had him transferred there."

"How long ago was this?"

"A year and a half or two years ago. He didn't like or trust the Germans, but he was fairly discreet about it. Then he began investigating something on his own that he was reluctant to talk about."

"You have no idea what it was?"

"It's my impression that he was beginning to think that there was either someone here at the Admiralty, or someone with access to our material, who wasn't entirely trustworthy and was passing on important information to the Germans."

"In other words, an enemy agent or spy."

"That's correct. Do you agree, Dixon?"

"I do. At least, that's the way I interpreted it."

"About six months ago he went off to the Baltic on a short holiday with his wife. He went out sailing one morning, and he never came back. Alive, that is."

"An accident?"

"We wondered about that too, because he was an extremely good swimmer and small boat sailor. But the Germans looked into it, and so did we, and everyone agreed that it had been a very stormy day and that the water was icy cold. Besides, when his body was recovered, there were no signs of foul play."

"I see. Now what about the captain's father? Does he come into the story, too?"

"He does indeed. He was in Africa at the time of the accident. He's something of an explorer as well as a naturalist, and he was trying to find the source of the Niger. He got back about a month ago, and when he heard what had happened, he came to see me. We told him everything we've told you in perhaps even greater detail because he questioned us very closely. Didn't he, Dixon?"

"He certainly did. But it was understandable. After all, the captain was his only son."

"Yes. Apparently, like the rest of us, he had some doubts as to whether what had happened was an accident; he implied that he might go to Germany to conduct his own investigation. And he did go, because a few days ago he sent telegrams to us and to his son's widow from Berlin saying that he'd discovered some very interesting things that he would tell us about when he got home. But something must have come up, because we haven't heard from him since, don't know where he is—"

"He's here," said Wyatt.

"Here in London?"

"Yes."

"How long has he been here?"

"Three or four days."

"But then why hasn't he been in touch with us?"

"Because he wasn't able to do anything, get in touch

with anyone. He apparently had a stroke—a very severe one—immediately after he got back to London, and he's been paralyzed, unable to speak ever since."

"Oh, no!" said Sir Arthur, his face showing his shock and concern. "But that's awful! Where is he?"

"At home. I understand that he's too ill to move. But an extremely good doctor has been attending him—Dr. Thurlow of Harley Street."

"Make a note of that, Dixon," said Sir Arthur. "I'd like to talk to him, find out what he believes Cortland's chances of recovery are."

"I've already done so," said Dixon, writing in a pocket notebook. "Would you now tell us why you're interested in all this, Inspector?"

"Of course. I've already told you that Andrew here is a friend of young Cortland's. They're at school together, came down to London together—Andrew a few days early because of illness in his house and Cortland because he was summoned home by a telegram. Andrew stopped by to see Cortland the next day, heard about the old gentleman's stroke and told me about it at lunch. His grandfather's illness, coming so soon after his father's death, upset young Cortland very much, and this in turn upset Andrew—upset him enough so that he asked me if I thought there could be more to what happened than met the eye."

"And do you think that?" asked Sir Arthur.

"I don't know how there could be. A stroke is a

stroke, and I suspect that Cortland Senior's was brought on by distress when he began looking into his son's death. You might ask Dr. Thurlow if that's not possible when you speak to him."

"I certainly will. What about you, Andrew? Do you still feel there's something wrong here?"

"If Inspector Wyatt doesn't, then of course I don't."

"And do you intend to pass on what you've heard—and what the inspector believes—to young Cortland?"

"If you've no objection to it."

"On the contrary. I think he needs all the reassurance he can get after everything that's happened. I'll get in touch with Dr. Thurlow, find out if I can see the old gentleman. But in the meantime, I'd like to meet young Cortland. Will you tell him that? Tell him to stop by here?"

"You won't be here, Sir Arthur," said Dixon. "Not if it's within the next week or so."

"What? Oh, you're right. I'll be going to Portsmouth for a very important meeting. But you'll be here, won't you, Dixon?"

"I will." He took a card from a case and wrote something on the back of it. "Here's my card, which you can give to young Cortland. If he presents it downstairs, they'll bring him right up here. And if he should want to see or should need me for any reason when I'm not here, I've written my home address on the back of the card."

"Thank you," said Andrew. "I think he'd like to meet you, talk to you both."

"And I thank you also," said Wyatt, getting up. "Both of you. I found everything you told us very interesting."

"You'll get in touch with Dr. Thurlow, let us know if there's any change in Cortland Senior's condition, won't you, Dixon?"

"I will indeed, Sir Arthur," said Dixon emphatically. "And I would like the Inspector to know how very important this matter is to us. Captain Cortland was one of our people. And if you have the slightest suspicion about what happened to him or to Cortland Senior—if you should change your mind and decide that you're going to look further into the matter—I urge you to let us know at once so that we can do anything we can to help you."

"I understand how you feel, Mr. Dixon," said Wyatt. "And those feelings do you credit."

He was clearly impressed by Dixon's vehemence, and Andrew was also—though that was not the whole story. They left, and neither of them said anything until they were outside, walking up Whitehall.

"Well?" said Andrew. "*Are* you going to look further into the whole thing?"

"Do you think I should?"

"Are you having me on? Don't you think there's something very rum about the whole thing? Cortland's father starts suspecting that there may be a spy either at the

Admiralty or the embassy in Berlin and he dies mysteriously. And when Cortland's grandfather starts looking into *his* death, he has a stroke. A stroke that may not *be* a stroke according to Dr. Reeves."

"That's right."

"I notice that you didn't say anything about that, what Dr. Reeves said about his condition. Nor did you tell them what he said to me when he communicated with me by blinking."

"No."

Andrew knew better than to continue this line of questioning, but he did ask something else.

"Dr. Reeves asked if you could get him to St. Mary's Hospital for a proper examination and better care than he's getting at home. And you said you'd see."

"Did I?"

"Yes."

"You think I can do anything I want, don't you?"

"Almost anything."

"Well, I can't. When you get older, you'll learn that the more authority you have, the more that authority is likely to be hedged round with restrictions."

"Are you saying you *can't* do anything about it?"

"What are you suggesting I do? Tell Mrs. Cortland that we don't approve of the way her father-in-law is being cared for and insist that she take him to a hospital?"

"No. I don't suppose you could do that."

"We certainly couldn't. Now be quiet and let me think."

They continued up Whitehall and reached the corner of Downing Street before Wyatt paused. Taking a notebook out of his pocket and leaning against a pillar box, he wrote something, tore out the page and folded it carefully.

"You haven't seen old Beasley since you got back to town, have you?"

"No."

"I think you should go see him. And when you do, tell him what happened when you saw Cortland's grandfather, how you feel about it and why."

"Tell him everything, including what Dr. Reeves said?"

"Yes. And when you've done that, give him this note." And he gave Andrew the folded note he had just written.

"All right," said Andrew. "I'll go see him right away."

"I would. If you hurry, he might take you to lunch. And that, as you know, is usually an experience."

6

Beasley

Andrew caught a red Westminster bus at Bridge Street, changed at Marble Arch, got off at Pembridge Road and walked to Beasley's shop on Portobello Road. It had changed little since Wyatt had taken him and Sara there for the first time. The same brass samovar was in the window, surrounded by glass paperweights and decorated china doorknobs. The marble head of Napoleon still frowned out at the world through the grimy glass. Beasley was there, sitting behind the counter, wearing the bottle green velvet jacket he usually wore in the shop. He was deep in conversation with a sturdy, sharp-featured man who wore an oversized flat cap and had a brightly colored neckerchief tied around his neck.

"Well, spring's early this year," said Beasley. "How goes, old chum?"

"Up and down like Tower Bridge," said Andrew, giving him the accepted response. "You're looking well."

"What else have I got to do?" Then, nodding to the man with the cap and the neckerchief, "Alf, my friend, Andrew. Andrew, my friend, Alf."

"Pleased to meet you." said Alf, taking stock of him with a quick, sweeping glance.

"And I'm happy to meet you," said Andrew.

"You do run to toffs, don't you?" said Alf, turning back to Beasley.

"I've never been proud," said Beasley. "If I was, what would I be doing with you."

"All right," said Alf. "No offense," he said to Andrew.

"Of course not."

"I'll be toddling, Baron. If I come across anything, I'll pass the word."

"Good-o. Kiss Liza for me."

"I'll do that." And nodding goodbye to Andrew, he left.

"Sorry if I interrupted anything," said Andrew.

"If you had, I'd have told you. Why aren't you at school?"

"Measles."

"You mean you've got 'em?"

"No." He explained. "But by now holidays will have started for everyone."

"How's Sara, and why isn't she with you?"

Andrew told him, and he whistled.

"Sara in a West End play—and with your mum at that! She must be proud as a monkey in mink!"

"She's very pleased. She didn't know I was coming here or she would have sent her love. And when she finds out I did come, she'll have forty fits."

"Aha! So you're here on some of old Wyatt's business!"

"Why do you say that?"

"I can't see you having something so important to talk to me about that it couldn't wait till she could come with you."

"Well, you're only partly right. The whole thing started as my problem. But Wyatt got interested in it and finally he told me to come and talk to you about it."

"I'm listening," said Beasley. Then, as Andrew glanced past him toward the back of the shop, "There's no one there but Sean doing some packing, and you know you can trust him like you do me."

So Andrew told him everything that had happened—told him much more, in fact, than Wyatt had told Sir Arthur and Dixon at the Admiralty. For, since he had not been instructed not to, he not only told Beasley about the way he had managed to communicate with Cortland's grandfather, but about Dr. Reeves' belief that the illness was not really a stroke.

Beasley, huge, pink and impassive as a Buddha, listened quietly.

"What am I supposed to do about it?" he asked when Andrew had finished.

"I don't know. But after I told you about it, I was supposed to give you this." And he gave him Wyatt's note.

Beasley read it with no more of a change of expression than he had exhibited while Andrew was talking.

"Fine," he said dryly when he had finished. "Lovely. In fact, enough to give your humble condumble the pip." Then, looking up, "Do they teach you Latin at that fancy school you're at?"

"Yes."

Opening a drawer under the counter, Beasley took out a slip of paper.

"Do you know what this means?" he asked, giving it to Andrew.

The few words on it, written with a strong hand in very black ink, read, "*Quid licet Jovis, non licet bovis.*"

"Yes. It means: That which is permitted to Jove, is not permitted to an ox. In other words, the god Jove can do things that an ox can't."

"Humph," said Beasley noncommittally. "Now turn it over."

On the other side, written in the same hand, was, "*Quid licet bovis, non licet Jovis.*"

"This is just the opposite. It means: An ox can do things that Jove can't." He looked up at Beasley. "Who gave you this?"

"Who do you think? His blinkin' nibs, Wyatt. And why? Because I'm the ox." He took the slip of paper back from Andrew. "Have you had lunch?"

"No."

"You're in luck. Neither have I." He rose. "Going out to lunch, Sean," he called. "Sell anything you like, but don't buy anything. Have 'em come back when I'm here."

"Yes, Mr. Beasley." He appeared from behind the curtain, a slim, redheaded young man in his early twenties. "Top of the morning to you, Andrew," he said.

"And to you, Sean."

"Where will you be if I need you, Mr. Beasley?"

"At the Russki's. Come on, Andrew."

They went out and up the street to a restaurant called The Russian Bear that was down a flight of steps in a cellar. Here Beasley was greeted by a man who was even bigger than he was and who was bearded to the eyes. He hugged Beasley, shook hands with Andrew, and recommended the borscht with piroshki, so that's what they had. Andrew knew that borscht was beet soup, but this turned out to have beef and cabbage in it as well. As for the piroshki, they were something like Cornish pasties— chopped meat in a light pastry crust—that you dipped into the borscht and ate along with it.

After a large bowl of the borscht and several piroshki, Andrew was full. Beasley had two bowls and many more piroshki and would probably have gone on to something else if Andrew had not been there, looking at him accusingly.

"What shall I tell Wyatt?" asked Andrew when they were outside.

"Tell him that you saw me and gave me his note," said Beasley.

"And that's all?"

"What else is there? Give Sara a Turkey rug for me."

Andrew was halfway to Notting Hill Gate before he realized that a Turkey rug must be rhyming slang for some kind of a hug, probably a hearty one.

Since he did not have anything to tell Wyatt, he decided not to go back to Scotland Yard. He was to meet his mother and Sara at the theatre and have dinner with them, but it was another nice day so he thought he'd walk. He went into Kensington Garden and strolled down the Broad Walk past Kensington Palace and the Round Pond, then walked east through Hyde Park, past the Serpentine, whose waters were becoming spring green after having been winter grey for so long. He left the park at Hyde Park Corner, walked down Picadilly, looking in the shop windows, and got to the theatre at a little before five.

Wyatt, looking gloomy, was coming out of the alley as Andrew turned into it, and after a quick glance at his long face, Andrew decided not to ask him what he was doing there. Instead, he told him that he'd seen Beasley and what Beasley had said; that he was merely to tell Wyatt that he *had* seen him. Wyatt nodded as if that was just about what he had expected and went up the Strand toward the Hotel Savoy.

Burke was at his post just inside the stage door. He greeted Andrew, told him that his mother and Sara were both still there and that they had just taken a break in the rehearsal so that, if he wanted to see them, this was a good time for it.

Andrew thanked him and went along into the wings. Verna was standing on the far side of the stage talking to Richards, the director. She waved to him, and he waved back, crossed the stage and went down the steps into the darkened theatre.

"Back here," called Sara. She was sitting near the back of the orchestra, and he went up the aisle and sat down next to her.

"How has it been going?" he asked.

"Pretty well. We've been working mostly on the second act today, and I have very little in it, so I haven't been doing much. What have you been up to?"

"Various things."

"Well, tell me. You said you would."

He did tell her. And of course there was a good deal to tell: about Dr. Reeves' feeling that there was something very strange about Cortland's grandfather's supposed stroke; about what they'd learned at the Admiralty; and about Andrew's visit to Beasley.

"What do you think Peter wanted him to do?" asked Sara.

"He didn't say. And, in any case, we're not sure he'll do it."

"Of course he'll do it. You know how he is. He always says he can't or won't do something, but in the end he always does."

"You mean he has so far."

"And I'm sure he will here. Because the more you've discovered about the case, the bigger and more important it seems."

"That's the way it looks to me, especially after what we learned at the Admiralty. I'm sure that Cortland's father was murdered. But I don't think Peter's really working on it, giving it his full attention."

"He probably isn't. You know about him, just as you do about Beasley. He always works on several cases at once."

"That's true. He was working on something when I went to see him at the Yard the other day. I don't suppose you know what it is."

"Of course I know."

"You mean he told you?"

"No. But he didn't have to."

"Why not?"

"Do you read the newspapers when you're away at school?"

"No. Just when I'm at home here in London."

"And then you read the *Times*, which hasn't said a great deal about it, though they've mentioned it. But it's been a really big story in all the other papers. And it's going to get even bigger, since the police haven't been able to do anything about it."

"What's 'it'?"

"The rash of robberies that they've been having around here during the last month or so."

"You don't mean burglaries, do you?"

"No, no. Pickpocket. Mostly in the theatre district. According to the papers, there have been three or four times as many as they've ever had before. And they expect that when more theatres open—us in a few weeks and the new Gilbert and Sullivan at the Savoy—it's going to get even worse."

"And you think that's what Peter's working on?"

"Yes, I do. Maybe not in the beginning when the papers began asking how the Yard could solve real crimes like murders when they couldn't round up a few pickpockets. But then a few M.P.'s began asking questions about it in the House, and finally, a little over a week ago, the Home Secretary got shirty about it and told the press they were making a fuss about nothing and the Yard would have the whole thing in hand in a few days."

Andrew whistled softly. "That wasn't very clever."

"No. Then the papers started going after *him*."

"And of course if things got really bad, that's when they'd call Peter in."

"It was right about then that I started seeing him around here, him and Sergeant Tucker. And he's been around almost every day since."

"Then you're probably right and that is what he's been working on. But why are they having so much trouble?"

"Do you know how pickpockets work?"

"Not really. I have an idea that they usually work in a crowd and bump into you to distract you while they pick your pocket."

"In other words, you think they work alone."

"Don't they?"

"A few of them may, but the best, most professional ones work in gangs of three or four. The first stall goes ahead, picks out the mark—the person to be robbed—and indicates him or her to the dip, the pickpocket. A second stall, walking with the dip, does the jostling or whatever is done to distract the mark. The pickpocket, called the dip or the tooler, makes the dip and passes whatever he's taken to a third stall, who immediately scarpers with it so that if the dip is collared, he's clean."

"How do you know so much about it?"

"How?" She went into her broadest Cockney. "Why do you think they used to call me Slippery Sara when I lived at Dingell's Court?" Then, as he smiled appreciatively, "I did learn a good deal about it then. But I ran into Sergeant Tucker right after the first newspaper stories came out, and he told me the rest."

"But I still can't understand why the police haven't been able to catch whoever's doing it. I mean, if they know how it's done . . ."

"They know how it's generally been done before this. And they also know all the best-known London pick-pockets. But none of them seem to be involved, and they claim that they don't know what's going on, how it's being worked either." She glanced sideways at Andrew. "I had an idea of something we could try if you're game. Something that might give us a clue about who's doing it."

"What's the idea?" She told him, and he thought about it for a minute. "I can see several reasons why it might not work. But I don't see how it would hurt to try it."

"You're game, then?"

"Yes. When do you want to try it?"

"Peter's having dinner with us tonight. Then your mother's going to Mr. Harrison's to meet some people, and Peter will be going somewhere too. How about then, after they both leave?"

"Sounds fine. We'll do it then."

7

Sara's Dodge

Though they had to wait for Wyatt to join them, it was still light when they left the theatre. They had decided to eat at Simpson's, and since it was so close, Verna told Fred they would walk and that he should get his own supper and meet her at the restaurant later.

They heard music, the wheezy strains of an accordion, as they walked up the alley, and when they reached the Strand, they saw a pair of buskers—a man and a woman—putting on a performance for the queue that was waiting to buy tickets at the theatre next door. The couple, clearly Cockneys, were both wearing their pearlies, clothes so covered with buttons you could barely see the cloth on which they were sewed. The woman, young and quite pretty, wore a large hat trimmed with ostrich feathers, and the man a flat cap. He was playing "After the Ball Was Over" on the accordion and singing the words in a pleasant baritone; the woman was doing a graceful dance.

Andrew thought there was something familiar about the man, and when they all stopped to watch the pair, he recognized him as Alf, whom he had met at Beasley's shop. That meant that the woman was probably Liza.

With a last, drawn-out chord, Alf stopped playing and went into his patter.

"Would you believe I only weighed a pound and a half when I was born?" he asked.

"A pound and a half?"

"That's right."

"Did you live?"

"Live? You should see me now!"

He played a few deliberately squawking chords as the crowd laughed appreciatively; the two did a few dance steps together, and then he said, "Do you like riddles?"

" 'Course I like riddles," said Liza, if that's who it was. "What's the riddle?"

"Can you spell blind pig in two letters?"

She thought hard about this, frowning as she danced in a circle around him. Then she shook her head.

"No, I can't. How do you spell blind pig in two letters?"

"P G, 'cause if it's got no I it must be blind." Then, with another series of chords that echoed the groans of the crowd, he said, "Well, that's enough of that. On with the consort." And he launched into the strongly ac·ented rhythm of "Ta-ra-ra-boom-de-ay!" dancing lightly with Liza at the same time.

"They're good," said Andrew as they went up the Strand toward Simpson's.

"Yes, they are," said Verna. "I used to do some busking when I was Sara's age. But not around here. I didn't have the nerve to work the West End."

"Are they here every night?"

"They have been since I've been coming here," said Sara.

"They're getting to be as much a part of the scene as the old gaslight in front of the Savoy," said Wyatt.

A constable who recognized him or Verna or both of them, raised a white-gloved hand and stopped the flow of hansoms, carriages and buses. And as they crossed to the southern side of the Strand, they heard another kind of music—the stirring strains of "Onward, Christian Soldiers"—and marching toward them from Waterloo Bridge came a small band in semi-military uniforms: dark blue with brass buttons, red shoulder tabs and red bands around their hats.

There were five of them in all, two women with earnest faces under their bonnets and three men wearing caps with shiny peaks. One woman carried a tambourine, which she shook and struck in time to the music and probably used to make collections. The other woman and one man played trumpets; a second man played a trombone; and bringing up the rear pounding a large bass drum was a plump, red-faced man who was so jolly-looking that he could have played Father Christmas without make-up.

Running along behind them, dancing and cavorting, were four or five ragged and dirty-faced urchins. And walking very sedately beside the band, pointedly ignoring the ragamuffins, was a nice-looking and very neat boy of about thirteen. His clothes, though not new, were clean and well-brushed, and from the possessive way he marched along beside the band, it was clear that he was related to one of the bandsmen.

"Salvation Army?" asked Andrew.

"No," said Wyatt. "They're Samaritans, very like the Salvation Army. In fact, there's been talk of their merging. They're around here a good deal, often stop and play in front of one of the theatres."

Whether the constable had or hadn't known Verna, she was certainly known at Simpson's, as she was at most West End restaurants, and they were given a choice corner table. When they had ordered, one of the carvers wheeled his huge shining cart over to the table and performed with his usual dexterity, giving each of them exactly the cut of beef he or she fancied.

It was a little before eight when they left, full of beef, Yorkshire pudding and trifle. Fred was waiting, and though Verna suggested that Sara and Andrew come along so that Fred could take them home after he had dropped her, they said that they would go home on their own. Verna went off and, as they had expected he would, so did Wyatt. They watched him stride off down the Strand, frowning in concentration and wearing what Sara called his working face.

They waited till he had disappeared in the hurrying throng of theatre-goers, some on foot, some getting out of hansoms and carriages, then they crossed the street and started back up the Strand themselves.

The whole area was alive now and at its busiest. The streetlights had been lit, and there were yellow pools of light around each standard. Women in satin and silk, men in shiny top hats and black and white evening clothes crowded the pavements. Alf and Liza were still performing in front of the theatre just up the street from the Windsor. As Sara and Andrew went down the alley to the stage door, they heard Alf begin to play "Champagne Charley," one of the current music hall favorites.

Burke was in his cubicle when they opened the door.

"Good evening, Miss Sara," he said in his hoarse voice. "Good evening, Master Andrew. Forget something?"

"Yes, I did," said Sara. "Do you want to wait here for me, Andrew? I won't be long."

Leaning against the door of the booth, Andrew talked to Burke. When he expressed surprise that the elderly doorkeeper was still there, Burke explained that when the play opened, he would have to be there until midnight, when the night watchman would take over. In the meantime, however, he was staying there that late, even though there was no need for it, so as to accustom himself to the hours and the routine. They then talked about racing and had just gotten around to discussing who they liked for the Derby when Sara, going by quickly, called good night to Burke and went out the stage door. Andrew said good night also and followed more slowly. His task had been to keep the doorkeeper busy, not let him see Sara when she left, and he must have been successful for Burke never commented.

And there was a good deal to comment about as Andrew realized when he got outside in the alley. For, instead of the pretty, neat and well-dressed girl that had entered the theatre, there was now a dirty-faced, unkempt and ragged street urchin, as disreputable as any of the ragamuffins they had seen marching alongside the Samaritan Band. Not that this was any surprise to Andrew, for he had seen her make this same transformation before, changing herself into the poor Cockney girl she had been when he first met her, and doing it without the grease paint and other theatrical aids that were now available to her in the theatre dressing room.

"Got your eye full?" asked Sara aggressively as he looked at her, repeating the first words she had ever said to him.

"Yes, I have," he said smiling.

"How do I look?"

"As if you haven't had a decent meal in a week and no bath for at least a month. Where shall we start?"

"Right here's as good as anyplace. I'll go up the alley and turn left on the Strand. If nothing happens by the time we get to Wellington Street, we'll call it off and try somewhere else."

"All right. How much of a start do you want?"

"Oh, ten yards or so."

"Right. Go ahead."

She started up the alley. When she was almost at the end of it, she began to run and Andrew started running after her, shouting, "Stop her! Stop, thief!"

She whipped around the corner; and when he reached the street, he caught a glimpse of her running fleetly and dodging in and out of the pedestrians.

"Get her!" he shouted again. "Stop, thief!"

He caught another glimpse of her as she reached the buskers—Alf still playing and Liza dancing—then she seemed to disappear. Surprisingly few people turned around or paid any attention to his shouts, either because they were too busy with their own concerns, hurrying to theatre, or because the traffic was making too much noise for them to hear them.

Andrew had reached the buskers now, too, and, still shouting, was trying to see where Sara had gone when something caught his foot and he tripped and fell. He just managed to catch himself so that though he went down on his hands and knees he was not hurt.

"Whoops-a-daisy! Careful there, me old brown son," said a nasal Cockney voice. "You've only got one neck, you know."

"I know," said Andrew. Someone helped him to his feet. Then, as he turned around,

"Well, blimey!" said Alf. "So it's you."

"Yes," said Andrew, brushing off his knees.

"You know him?" said Liza, who was now standing off to one side near a building.

"Yus. He's a friend of Beasley's." Then, as a thought struck him, "And Inspector Wyatt's, too?"

"Yes. What happened to Sara, do you know?"

"You mean her?" asked Liza. She stepped aside, and there, behind her in the shadowy side door of a closed shop, was Sara.

"Are you all right?" Andrew asked her.

Sara nodded. And as Andrew realized what had happened—that Alf had tripped him and Liza had hidden Sara to help her escape—what it meant became clear to Alf, too.

"Are you barmy?" he asked angrily. "What kind of giddy game are you up to?"

"We were trying to help him out," said Sara in a subdued voice. "The inspector, I mean."

"You're not helping anyone sticking your sneezer into something that's none of your business! Now get out of this!"

They walked slowly back to the alley and along it to

the stage door. Sara couldn't go home as she was, so Andrew went in first and told Burke he had fallen—which of course was true—and asked if he could clean himself up a bit. Burke couldn't have been more sympathetic; and while he was helping Andrew brush off his clothes, Sara slipped past him and went to her dressing room. Andrew and Burke continued their discussion of their choices for the Derby, and Andrew had just finished explaining that while he wasn't an expert, their coachman, Fred, was, when Sara, once more tidy, rejoined them.

They thanked Burke, went out and up the alley. When they reached the street, they paused, for there, looking like a thundercloud, was Wyatt.

"What the blazes have you two been up to?" he asked.

This time it was Andrew who responded, giving him the same answer that Sara had given Alf.

"We were trying to help," he said. "We knew you were after the pickpockets who've been working around here."

"Well?"

"Sara dressed like a street urchin and started running, and I ran after her yelling, 'Stop, thief!' as if she'd pinched my purse."

"And exactly how was that supposed to help?"

"We thought," said Sara, "if anyone from the gang was around and saw me, one of two things would happen. Either they'd ask me to join them, work with them, or they'd get mad and tell me this was their pitch and to clear out or they'd bash me."

"I see. I gather you think you're a little smarter than anyone on the Metropolitan Police force."

"Not really."

"No? Then perhaps you're willing to admit that we've thought of everything you can think of to collar them and perhaps a few things you haven't."

"We're sorry, Peter," said Sara. "We really weren't trying to interfere."

"Well, that's what you were doing. I'm not saying that you haven't been helpful in the past. But when you go off on your own like this, not knowing what we've been doing or what we're up against . . . You said that whoever's working around here might bash you. Do you know what that means? How badly they might hurt you?"

"I think so."

"I doubt it. But even if it wasn't as bad as it might be, how do you think I'd feel about it?"

"All right," said Andrew. "We get the idea. We're sorry, and we won't do it again. But . . . How did you know what happened?"

"How do you think?"

"Alf and Liza told you. Are they working with you?"

"Stop asking questions about things that are none of your business. How are you getting home?"

"We'll take a bus."

"No, you won't."

He hailed a hansom, put them in it and gave the cabby their address. Then, though Andrew protested, he dropped the money to pay for it in Sara's lap and stood there while the hansom took them off.

8

The Ox Performs

A telegram came for Andrew at about nine the next morning. Sara was having breakfast with him when Matson brought it in, and though she looked out the window with pretended indifference when he opened it, he knew that she was watching him out of the corner of her eye.

When he had finished it, he handed it to her and she read, "If still interested in matter you saw me about, urge your presence at Sherburne Square at nine tonight." It was signed, The Ox.

"Isn't Sherburne Square where your friend Cortland lives?"

"Yes."

"Who's The Ox?"

"Beasley."

"Why?"

He told her about the Latin phrases Beasley had shown him.

"What's he up to?"

"I don't know, but it's got to have something to do with either Cortland or his grandfather."

"I take it you're going."

"Of course. Do you want to come with me?"

She looked at him steadily. "If you hadn't shown me the telegram, I would have thrown the teapot at you. If you hadn't asked me to come, I would have thrown the teapot *and* the milk jug."

"Lucky I did then," he said, grinning. "There won't be any trouble about it, will there? I mean, you don't have a rehearsal, do you?"

"No. And your mother's going to be out. She's going to a concert at St. James Hall with Mr. Richards and his wife."

"That's good."

They both knew that Verna would probably have let them go out if they had wanted to, but she would also have asked a few questions that they might have had difficulty in answering.

In the light of Beasley's telegram, it did not seem wise to go to see Cortland when Sara and his mother went off to the theatre that afternoon. And, after the dressing down that Wyatt had given them the night before, Andrew thought he had better stay away from the Yard.

What should he do, then? He suddenly remembered

that one of the things he and Chadwick had talked about when they were coming down from school was Maskelyne, the famous stage magician. Chadwick said he had never seen him and was interested to hear that Andrew had several times. That seemed worth a try, so he had Fred drop him off on Picadilly when he was driving Verna and Sara to the theatre. He took a bus back to Belgravia, found Chadwick in and delighted at the idea of seeing Maskelyne, especially with Andrew, so they went to the Egyptian Hall and spent the afternoon watching magic tricks and illusions that impressed Chadwick more than he cared to admit, though he spent some time after they left the theatre making guesses as to how the various tricks were done and seemed disappointed when Andrew said he had no more idea about them than Chadwick did.

Mr. and Mrs. Richards picked Verna up a litttle before eight to take her to the concert, and shortly after that Andrew remarked that it was a nice night and asked Sara's mother if it was all right if they went out for a walk. Mrs. Wiggins, busy bringing the household accounts up to date, said, "Of course." That it was a good idea after they'd both spent the afternoon in stuffy theatres, but not to come home too late, and they said they wouldn't.

They took their time walking to Sherburne Square, pausing on the bridge over the Regent's Canal until

Andrew looked at his watch and said they'd better stir stumps, so they walked the rest of the way quite briskly. The bells of St. John's were just striking nine when they arrived at the Square.

"Where's your friend's house?" asked Sara.

Andrew pointed it out to her.

"Where's Beasley?"

"I've no idea."

"He did say nine, didn't he?"

"Yes. Now be patient. He may not come here himself, but if he said I was to be here—"

Sara clutched his arm. "Look!" she said excitedly.

A plume of smoke drifted out of the iron gate under the steps of the Cortland house and more smoke puffed out of the partly open basement window.

"Fire!"

"Yes. And here comes Beasley."

If they had not been expecting him, they might not have recognized him, for he was dressed, not as he usually was in his bottle green velvet jacket, but in the dark, sober clothes of a butler or a valet on his day off. To complete the picture, he wore a bowler that sat squarely on his head with no nonsense of tipping it forward, back or to either side.

Moving with a lightness that was surprising in such a big man, he ran up the steps of the Cortland house, tugged at the bell-pull and kept tugging at it. Andrew and Sara moved closer and were near the foot of the steps when the door opened and Hodge looked out.

"Are you all asleep in there?" said Beasley severely. "Don't you know what's going on?"

"What?"

"Look there!" said Beasley, pointing to the smoke. "Fire! And a bad one, I suspect. I've already sent for the brigade. Better get everyone out of the house."

"But . . . but . . ."

"Don't argue, man! I'm telling you to get everyone out! It could be a matter of life or death!" Then, leaning past Hodge, he shouted up the stairs. "Fire! Fire! Everyone out of the house! And hurry!"

By now windows were opening in other houses on the square. Doors were opening, and householders and servants were peering out.

"All right," said Hodge. "The madam's out, but cook and the maids is upstairs and so's the boy. I'll get them." And he hurried back inside and up the stairs, leaving the door open. Beasley came down the stairs and stood there, near Sara and Andrew, but with his back to them.

"Where is he?" he asked under his breath and without turning around.

Andrew knew he must mean Cortland's grandfather.

"To the right at the top of the stairs," he said.

Beasley nodded and bent down, peering at the smoke that was much thicker now, pouring out of the basement gate and the partly open window.

"It's good one, all right. Hot enough to smoke haddocks. And here come the brave fire laddies."

Horses galloping and sparks streaming from the stack of the steam pumper, the fire brigade arrived. As they jumped down off their engines, trim and military in their shining brass helmets, blue uniforms and boots, young Cortland came down the outside steps of the house, followed by a plump woman—probably the cook—and the maids and tweeny. They must have been in bed or getting ready for bed, for they were all in wrappers or had blankets or shawls over their shoulders. But while Cortland's hair was a bit touseled, he was fully dressed and, for some reason, he did not seem at all surprised to see Andrew there.

"What's happening?" he asked.

"Fire," said Andrew. "Didn't Hodge tell you?"

"He did say something about it, but I wasn't sure . . ." Then, in a belated reaction, "Fire? What about my grandfather?"

"Not to worry," said Beasley. Then, authoritatively, "Here, men. We've got a sick old man upstairs who can't get around on his own. Two of you get him while the rest of you take care of the fire."

Two of the sturdiest of the firemen immediately ran up the steps and into the house, while the others began to unroll their hoses and take them down into the basement.

"Is it a bad fire?" asked Cortland.

"I don't think anyone knows yet," said Andrew. "By the way, this is Sara Wiggins. I've told you about her."

"Yes, you have," said Cortland.

"Hello," said Sara. "Is everyone out of the house now?"

"Everyone except grandfather. My stepmother went out some time ago. I believe she's having dinner with Dr. Thurlow and . . . Oh. They did get grandfather!"

They watched as the firemen came carefully down the steps. They had wrapped Mr. Cortland in a blanket and were carrying him between them, each of them holding one of his legs but supporting his back so that he was sitting bolt upright.

Cortland hurried over to him.

"Grandfather, are you all right?" he asked anxiously.

The old gentleman's eyes went to his face, then moved right and left, taking in as much of the scene as he could.

"*Is* he all right?" asked Sara.

"He seems to be. He's had a stroke, so he can't talk. But what are we going to do with him? He can't stay out here in the street, and . . ."

"Of course not," said Beasley. "And here's the ambulance."

Its bell ringing, the ambulance drew up near one of the fire engines, and the driver and the attendant jumped down.

"Here you are," called Beasley. "Here's your patient."

The driver and attendant took a stretcher out of the

ambulance, the two firemen carried Mr. Cortland over to it and laid him down gently. The driver and attendant covered him with another blanket, strapped him down, put the stretcher back inside the ambulance again, and not more than a minute or two after it had arrived, it was on its way back to the hospital.

"Well, that's that. Smartly done," said Beasley.

Andrew agreed silently, especially when the door of a four-wheeler that had followed the ambulance opened and Beasley's assistant, Sean, looked out. He must have gone to the hospital and summoned the ambulance while Beasley was calling the fire brigade.

Hodge, standing further up the street with the cook and the maids, watched the ambulance go off. Then, saying something to the cook, went hurrying up the street himself.

"Nothing more to be done here," said Beasley, "so we might as well be going. Can we take you anywhere?" he asked Sara and Andrew.

"What are you going to do now?" Andrew asked Cortland.

"I don't know. I suppose I should stay and see how bad the fire is, but I'm much more concerned about my grandfather. Do you know what hospital they've taken him to?"

"Of course," said Beasley. "St. Mary's. Get in, and we'll take you there."

Sean stepped aside; Sara, Andrew and Cortland got

into the cab; Beasley said something to the cabby, then he and Sean got into the four-wheeler too, sitting opposite the three young people.

"Do you think it's a bad fire?" asked Sara.

"I shouldn't think so," said Beasley. "You know the old saying?"

"You mean, 'Where there's smoke, there's fire.'?"

"Yes. Like many of the old things they say, it's not always true."

"I see," said Sara, smiling.

"Do you know each other?" asked Cortland, looking from Sara and Andrew to Beasley.

"Now that's a question," said Beasley with great gravity. "Can any man truly say he knows another? You're a bit of a scholar, Sean. What do you think?"

"Much too deep and difficult a question for me, Mr. Beasley," said Sean. "I wouldn't dream of trying to answer it."

"Oh," said Cortland, with a gleam in his eye. "The next thing I was going to ask was how you happened to be there, Tillett—you and Miss Wiggins—when the fire broke out. But perhaps I'd better not."

"It's always better not to," said Beasley. "The fewer questions you ask, the fewer lies you'll be told."

"You don't think very much of people, do you?" said Sara.

"You run a shop like mine for a while, and see what you think of them. Shoful, almost everyone—meaning no good, fake. Buying or selling, they'll cheat you out of your eyeteeth if they can. True, Sean?"

"I've never seen anyone get the better of you, Mr. B., either buying or selling. But, in a general way, I suppose it's true."

"Where are we now?" asked Cortland, peering out through the window.

"Praed Street," said Beasley. "Almost there."

The growler turned into Norfolk Place and drew up in front of the hospital.

"There you are," said Beasley, opening the cab door. "The best of British luck to you."

"Thank you," said Cortland, getting out. "Thank you very much for everything."

"Nothing to it. Delighted to have been of service. Ta-ta, chums."

Beasley shut the cab door, and it went off.

The three went through the large battered doors and into the reception hall. It was the first time any of them had been in a hospital, and its size awed them. The clerk at the admissions desk, used to odd occurrences, did not seem particularly surprised to see three young people appear at that hour without an adult accompanying them, but he did not know anything about Cortland's grandfather, and it took some time before the messenger he sent to Emergency came back with information.

They were directed upstairs, where the sister in charge told them that, yes, Mr. Cortland was there and Dr.

Reeves was with him; and if they would sit down on that bench there, the doctor would talk to them.

"You're behind all this, aren't you?" asked Cortland as they sat.

"Do you think so?" said Andrew.

"Yes. I'm still not sure exactly how you did it, but I know that somehow you were talking to Grandfather when you were last at the house."

"I did it by telling him to blink."

"Blink?"

"Yes." Andrew explained, and Cortland nodded as if that was exactly the kind of thing he would expect Andrew to do. They continued to sit there on the bench, watching the sister work at her desk and the nurses going back and forth into the wards, until finally the door of a room some distance up the corridor opened and Dr. Reeves, the doctor Andrew had met with Wyatt, came down the corridor toward them. Though it was quite late, he was as dapper as ever. He nodded to Andrew, said to Cortland, "You're Benedict Cortland's grandson?"

"Yes, I am. How is my grandfather?"

"I'm not sure I know how to answer that," he began. He broke off, looking up the corridor at the sound of rapid footsteps. Andrew, Sara and Cortland looked up the corridor, too; and there, walking toward them quickly, were Cortland's stepmother and Dr. Thurlow. They were both in evening clothes, Mrs. Cortland wearing a green silk dress and pearls, and Dr. Thurlow with a cape thrown over his shoulders.

"I'm relieved to see you, Benedict," said Mrs. Cortland. "We weren't sure where you'd gone. Is your grandfather here?"

"Yes, he is."

"You're young Cortland's mother?" said Dr. Reeves.

"His stepmother. And you?"

"I'm Dr. Reeves."

"Oh. How do you do. This is Dr. Thurlow."

"Yes, I know. I've had the pleasure of hearing Dr. Thurlow lecture." Then, as Dr. Thurlow bowed in acknowledgement, "How did you know that Mr. Cortland was here?"

"My butler knew that I was having dinner with Dr. Thurlow, and when the ambulance took Mr. Cortland away, he came to tell me what had happened."

"How is he?" asked Dr. Thurlow.

"It's difficult to say. He appears to have had a stroke or some sort of seizure, so that he can't talk, can't really communicate."

"Yes, I know. I've been taking care of him."

"Oh, have you?"

"Yes, I have."

Andrew watched the confrontation between the two doctors with fascination. For although he was not sure he understood everything that was going on—and of course they were both being very polite—there was no doubt in his mind that it *was* a confrontation. The way in which Dr. Reeves had seen the old gentleman before was such that Andrew could understand why he could not admit that he *had* seen him or that he knew that Dr. Thurlow had been attending him. But why was Dr. Thurlow being so tentative? This must have puzzled Mrs. Cortland too, for after a glance at him, she said to Dr. Reeves, "I gather that someone who wasn't familiar wtih the circumstances felt it was necessary to bring him here, but we've come to take him home."

"I'm afraid that's impossible, Mrs. Cortland."

She drew herself up. "What do you mean by impossible?"

"I mean I cannot permit him to be moved. As. Dr. Thurlow will testify—*must* testify if he has been taking care of him—Mr. Cortland was in a precarious state of health as it was. On top of that, he was exposed to a fire, to possible smoke inhalation and to transportation here—all of which must have had a profound effect on his nervous system. In the light of all this, I'm sure that Dr. Thurlow will agree that he should not be moved again. Certainly not tonight."

"I'm not certain about that," said Dr. Thurlow.

"Well, I am," said Dr. Reeves. "I would not want to take the responsibility for releasing him now, after what he has been through, especially when he can have all the attention he needs here, while . . . have you had a nurse taking care of him at home?"

Mrs. Cortland and Dr. Thurlow both looked at young Cortland. They had no way of knowing whether he'd told Dr. Reeves that there *hadn't* been a nurse taking care of him, and they couldn't take a chance on lying.

"No," said Dr. Thurlow. "No, we didn't. I didn't think it was necessary because Mrs. Cortland was spending a great deal of time with him, and he seemed to be improving."

"Well, if he has been improving, he's lost a good deal of ground, and I will not permit him to be moved again, certainly not tonight."

"But . . ." Mrs. Cortland began.

"Perhaps it might be better to let him remain here tonight, Mrs. Cortland," said Dr. Thurlow smoothly. "If he's better tomorrow—or even if he's no worse—I'm sure Dr. Reeves will be willing to release him to your very capable hands."

"If you think that's best," she said with ill-concealed annoyance, "very well." Then, looking at Andrew, "What's your friend Tillett doing here, Benedict?"

"Keeping me company," said Cortland before Andrew could answer, even decide what he should say. "He and his friend, Miss Wiggins, were passing by when the fire broke out, and when they saw whose house it was, they stayed to see if there was anything they could do to help."

"Very kind of them," said Mrs. Cortland without much conviction. "All right. We'll go. Come along, Benedict. But I'll be back tomorrow morning, Doctor."

"By all means," said Dr. Reeves, bowing. "And I hope I'll be able to give you a better report on Mr. Cortland's condition then than I have now."

"I hope so, too," said Mrs. Cortland. "But I'm telling you now that no matter what you say, I intend to take him back home with me where he belongs!" She went off with Dr. Thurlow walking beside her and young Cortland a step or two behind.

Dr. Reeves, Andrew and Sara watched them go, then looked at one another. Dr. Reeves' face was expressionless, and in the light of that, Andrew decided not to comment on what had happened.

"How are you two going to get home?" asked Dr. Reeves.

"Probably take a hansom," said Andrew.

"No need for that," said the doctor. "My carriage is downstairs. You know it, don't you?"

"Yes," said Andrew.

"Well, I'm going to be here for a while yet. I want to take another look at Mr. Cortland. Tell my coachman to take you home and then come back here for me."

"Thank you very much," said Andrew.

Dr. Reeves dismissed his thanks with a wave of his hand and went back up the corridor to Mr. Cortland's room.

9

The Hospital

Andrew went back to Sherburne Place at about ten o'clock the following morning. Sara had an early rehearsal so she could not go with him, but she made him promise that he would come to the theatre as soon as he could and tell her what happened.

It was lucky that Andrew got there when he did, for when he turned into the street, he saw that a carriage was waiting in front of the house, and as he approached it, the door opened and Cortland and his stepmother came out and started down the steps. Andrew hurried toward them.

"Good morning," he said to Mrs. Cortland. "I was very worried about Cortland's grandfather, and I wondered how he was this morning."

"We don't know," said Mrs. Cortland shortly. "We're on our way over to the hospital now to find out."

"Would you like to come with us?" asked Cortland with barely concealed eagerness.

"Why, thank you. I have some things to do later on, but . . . Yes, I'd like to come. I know how fond of him you are, and as I said, I was quite concerned about him."

"Come along, then," said Mrs. Cortland not too graciously.

The coachman had descended from the box and was holding the carriage door open. She got in.

"St. Mary's Hospital," she said.

The coachman saluted. Andrew and Cortland got in. The coachman closed the door, climbed back into the box, cracked his whip, and they went off.

It was, on the whole, a silent drive. Mrs. Cortland sat there, lips compressed and frowning, until they had almost reached Praed Street. Cortland was quiet at first also, looking out the window rather than at his stepmother. But he finally asked a few questions about Sara, and when Mrs. Cortland heard that she was in the play with Andrew's mother, she began to exhibit a little interest, asked who else was in it, when it was opening and the other things that people usually asked.

They went in the hospital's Norfolk Street entrance and up the stairs to the ward where they had been the night before.

There was a different sister at the desk this time. Mr. Cortland might be a little better this morning, she told Cortland's stepmother. In any case, he was no worse, did not seem to have suffered too much as a result of the fire.

"That's good," said Mrs. Cortland. "Becauses I've come to take him home."

The sister looked at her in astonishment. "That's impossible," she said.

"Is it?"

"Of course. He's in no condition to go home. And, in any case, Dr. Reeves left no instructions that he was to be permitted to leave."

"Did he not?" Mrs. Cortland's normally fair skin was becoming flushed. "That's too bad. I am, in any case, taking him."

"I repeat, that's impossible," said the sister firmly.

"Are you saying that you intend to keep him here against his will?"

"Since he's unable to speak, we don't know what his will is in this matter and must rely on Dr. Reeves' opinion of what is best for him."

"And that's your final word?"

"I'm afraid it is."

"Well, we'll see about that! Who is your superior? Who is the chief official here at the hospital?"

"That would be Dr. Pinkham. His office is downstairs."

"Very well." Her face no longer flushed, but white with rage, she turned to Cortland and Andrew. "Wait here. I'll be back."

Andrew and Cortland watched her go down the stairs,

then went over to the bench against the wall and sat down. As the sound of Mrs. Cortland's footsteps died away, a door behind the sister opened, and Wyatt came out.

"Well done, sister," he said. Then to Andrew, "I was quite sure that irate lady would come back this morning, and I rather suspected you'd manage to come along with her. Is this your friend?"

"Yes. Benedict Cortland, Third. Inspector Peter Wyatt."

"Hello," said Wyatt. "Nice to meet you."

"It's very nice to meet you, sir. How is my grandfather?"

"Dr. Reeves is in with him now, but what the sister told your stepmother was the truth. He does seem a bit better this morning."

"Oh, I'm glad. I've been very worried about him."

"I know you have. I also know you've had a feeling for some time that something very odd, even sinister, has been going on."

"Yes, I have. That's why I was so delighted when Tillett became interested in what was happening and spoke to you about it."

"Good. I understand that you were with your stepmother and Dr. Thurlow when they left here last night."

"Yes, I was."

"What did they talk about?"

"Mostly about what had just happened. They were

both furious that they couldn't take grandfather home. Though Dr. Thurlow didn't say as much as my stepmother, he was just as angry—perhaps even more so. When she said something about how she would have expected him to be able to do something about it since he was a doctor and supposedly a very well known one, he turned on her and shut her up, saying she didn't know anything about medical protocol or hospital procedure. Then they both looked at me and quieted down a little, and she said she'd go back there this morning."

"Anything else?"

"I don't think so." He thought a minute. "They said that there was something very odd about the fire, which wasn't at all serious, and they were going to ask Hodge about it, how it had started and who had called the fire brigade. And when we got home, they sent me up to bed and . . . Well, as I started up the stairs, I heard them saying something about a dispatch box."

"Ah! Do you know what they meant?"

"No."

"Do you know what a dispatch box is?"

"Yes. When my father was alive, he would occasionally get one from the Admiralty or the embassy or send one off. They were red metal boxes with the royal seal on them for important official papers."

"That's right. You haven't seen one around the house since you came home?"

"No, I haven't."

"All right. Now, your stepmother will be coming back here again soon. I don't know what she'll do next: either go to see Dr. Thurlow again or consult with a solicitor, probably. I doubt that she'll want you with her, but in any case, if you can possibly get away from her, do so and come back here. Clear?"

"Yes, sir."

"Until later, then." And nodding to them, he went off along the corridor to the room Dr. Reeves had come out of the night before.

They had gotten up and moved away from the sister's desk when they talked to Wyatt. Now they went back to the bench and sat down again.

"So that's the inspector," said Cortland. "I hoped I'd meet him some day."

"What did you think of him?"

"He seemed very nice and very intelligent. He doesn't look anything like what I thought he would, though."

"I said the same thing the first time I saw him in mufti, and he said, 'What's an inspector supposed to look like—an off-duty policeman with thick soles to his boots and a terrible hat that he never takes off?' "

"Of course. I never thought of it, but the less he looks like a policeman, the better."

A few moments later Mrs. Cortland came up. They did not have to ask her whether she had accomplished anything in her discussion with the hospital authorities.

If she had been angry before, she was now in a towering rage.

"If they think that's the end of this," she announced, "they're very much mistaken! I'm going to see my solicitor! Benedict, you go home."

Cortland glanced quickly at Andrew.

"Would you mind very much," he asked, "if instead of that, I do something with Tillett?"

"Do what?"

"It's another nice day," said Andrew. "We could go over to Regent's Park and take a boat out on the lake."

"Very well," said Mrs. Cortland, and it was clear that she was no longer thinking of her stepson but of where she was going and what she was going to do. "But be sure that you're home in time for tea."

"Yes, ma'am," said Cortland.

She went down the stairs, and they followed a bit more slowly. When they went out the door onto Norfolk Street, she had already gotten into the carriage and it was on its way toward Praed Street.

"Shall we go back now?" asked Cortland.

"Let's make sure she's really gone," said Andrew.

They walked to the corner. The carriage seemed to be still going east toward Marylebone Road, but to make sure, they walked completely around the west wing of the hospital before they went in and upstairs again.

"Oh, there you are," said the sister when they approached her desk. "Dr. Reeves is waiting for you. This way." And she led them along the corridor to the room. She tapped lightly on the door, opened it to let them in, then returned to her desk.

Old Mr. Cortland, propped up high with pillows, was in the bed. Dr. Reeves, his stethoscope hanging around his neck, was on one side of the bed, and Wyatt was on the other. Mr. Cortland's eyes went from his grandson's face to Andrew's, then back to young Cortland's again. His own face, though no more mobile and expressive than it had been, did not seem quite as tense and strained as it had.

"Hello," said Wyatt. "Has she gone?"

"Yes," said Andrew. "To see her solicitor. Or so she said."

"Good," said Wyatt. "I know you know my young friend, Andrew Tillett," he said to the doctor. "Do you also know young Cortland?"

"Yes," said Dr. Reeves. "We met last night."

"How is my grandfather?" asked Cortland. "The sister said that he was a little better today."

"He is. He seems to be regaining some sensation and even some mobility in his extremities. And while he still can't talk, he has been making a few sounds. Isn't that true, sir?" he asked the old man.

Mr. Cortland made a kind of growling noise deep in his throat.

"Oh, I am glad," said young Cortland, going to the

bed and pressing his hand. "I've been very worried about you, Grandfather."

Mr. Cortland made another slight noise that could have been an acknowledgement.

"I've already told you who I am, sir," said Wyatt. "I'm Inspector Wyatt of Scotland Yard. I think you know that I'm indirectly responsible for getting you here to the hospital. There are some things it's quite important that we find out. I thought I'd wait until your grandson got here before we began, but now . . . Do you feel up to answering a few questions?"

Mr. Cortland made a very brief sound and blinked.

"Good. I was going to suggest that we use the same system you used with my young friend, Andrew. One blink for yes. Two for no. Is that agreeable?"

Mr. Cortland blinked once.

"Splendid. Now when your grandson went home last night with your son's widow and Dr. Thurlow, he heard them talking about a dispatch box. Do you know what they meant?"

Again Mr. Cortland blinked once.

"You do know? Very good. Now this is going to be very difficult, and it's probably going to take several questions to arrive at an answer, but . . . Can you tell us what's in the dispatch box?"

Mr. Cortland made another, more extended noise, and he blinked—not once or twice—but five or six times.

"I'm sorry. I gather that's a question you can't answer with a simple yes or no. So let's try another one. Do you know where the dispatch box is?"

Mr. Cortland made another, even more extended noise and blinked five or six times. Dr. Reeves, who had picked up the old man's wrist and was taking his pulse, frowned.

"Just a second, Wyatt," he said. Slipping the earpieces of his stethoscope into his ears, he listened to Mr. Cortland's chest. "I'm sorry," he said. "I'm afraid I can't let you ask him any more questions. He's getting too excited, and it's too much of a strain."

"Right," said Wyatt. "I'm sorry if I upset you, sir," he said to the old man. "Please try to relax. I have the case in hand. I have a fairly good idea of what it's about, and I intend to see it through. In the meantime, I promise that I'll keep my eye on your grandson and make sure that no harm comes to him. Does that help any?"

The old man blinked once, then closed his eyes wearily and seemed to go to sleep.

"All right," said the doctor. "Out you go, all of you."

He opened the door, and they all went out. A nurse, trim and capable looking in her white cap and starched uniform, was waiting in the corridor. Reeves summoned her with a jerk of his head, gave her some instructions in an undertone, and she nodded and went into the room.

"I hope I didn't do him any harm," said Wyatt.

"I don't think you did," said the doctor. "But I was afraid you might if you continued. His pulse rate was going up, probably from frustration because you were asking questions he wanted to answer but couldn't."

"That's the impression I got. And of course that in itself is useful. Now can you tell us anything about his condition? You said you wanted to wait until young Cortland got here before you did."

"Yes." He looked at Cortland. "You were told that he was suffering from a stroke?"

"Yes. By my stepmother and by Dr. Thurlow."

"Well, I'm a little surprised at Thurlow. Because I don't think it was a stroke."

"That's what you said when you first saw him at home," said Wyatt. "Are you sure now?"

"Fairly sure. Many of the symptoms don't fit. But the most interesting one is the fact that, as I told you, sensation seems to be returning to his extremities—his toes, for instance—and he's even able to move them a little. This might happen in time if it were a stroke, but not so quickly."

"Do you have any idea what might have caused his condition?"

Dr. Reeves hesitated. "Possibly. I can't prove it, but . . . Do you know what curare is?"

"It's a poison that the South American Indians use, isn't it?"

"Yes. It's a powerful alkaloid that arrests the action of the motor nerves, which of course would induce paralysis. Detlow in Germany has been doing some interesting work with it, trying to determine if it can be used as an anesthetic. And . . . well, as I said, I can't prove it, but it occurred to me that if someone was injected with exactly the right dose in exactly the right place, he might develop the symptoms that Mr. Cortland has."

"If that's true, will he recover?"

"Yes. That's another reason it occurred to me as a possibility. Because, though it can cause almost instantaneous death when it is used as a poison, when it is used in smaller doses as a drug, its effects wear off quite rapidly."

"I see," said Wyatt. "Will you excuse me for a moment?"

Sergeant Tucker had come up the stairs and was standing near the sister's desk, waiting. Wyatt went over to him, and Tucker gave him a note, which he read with a good deal of interest.

"I don't really have anything more to say, and I do have some other patients to look at," said Dr. Reeves to Andrew. "So will you tell the inspector that if he wants me for anything else, he can find me either here or at my surgery?"

"Yes, sir," said Andrew.

"As for your grandfather," he said to Cortland, "if I'm correct in my guess as to the cause of his condition, I can virtually promise you that he'll be himself again within a few days."

"Thank you, sir. Thank you very much indeed," said Cortland.

"Not at all," said the doctor, and he went up the corridor and disappeared into an open ward. Tucker caught Andrew's eye and winked at him, and taking this—if not as an invitation—at least as an indication that nothing secret was going on, Andrew went over to them.

"You're sure about this?" Wyatt was asking.

"Yes, sir. Pearson sent us the word on it, and he's very reliable."

"Yes, he is." Wyatt turned and saw Andrew and young Cortland. "I don't believe you know Andrew's friend, Benedict Cortland, Third, do you, Sergeant? This is *my* friend and right hand, Sergeant Tucker."

"It's nice to meet you, Sergeant."

"It's a pleasure to meet any friend of Andrew's," said Tucker. "He gives us a lot of trouble, but we're still glad to have him around."

Wyatt looked at the note Tucker had given him again, then looked at Andrew and Cortland.

"Do the two of you have anything important planned for the rest of the morning?" he asked.

"No," said Andrew. "Why?"

"If you haven't, you might want to come and pay a visit with me."

"To whom? Where?"

"Sir Arthur Barry at the Admiralty."

10

The Admiralty Again

The same commissionaire was on duty at the Admiralty, and he must have remembered Wyatt, for though Wyatt did not have an appointment, he summoned a page and sent him up to Sir Arthur's office with Wyatt's card. The page came down almost immediately, saying that Sir Arthur would be happy to see the inspector, and led them back up to his office.

This time one of the clerks, a much younger man than Dixon, opened the door for them, and Sir Arthur himself came out to usher them into his office.

"Delighted to see you again, Inspector," he said. "You too, Andrew. As for this young man here, you don't have to tell me who he is. You're young Cortland, aren't you?"

"Yes, Sir Arthur."

"I'd know you anywhere. You look remarkably like

your father and also your grandfather, especially around the eyes."

"Thank you, sir."

"I'm glad you realize that's a compliment. Your father was a very striking-looking man. And your grandfather still is."

"I think so too, sir."

"I hope you didn't mind our dropping in like this with no warning," said Wyatt. "As a matter of fact, I wasn't sure you'd be here."

"Because of the Portsmouth meeting? I'm on my way there this afternoon. Dixon's out getting together all the papers I'll need to take with me."

"How long will you be gone, sir?"

"Three or four days."

"Then I'm glad we were able to catch you."

"So am I. I'm delighted to have a chance to meet young Cortland, and I'm hoping you have some good news for me about his grandfather. How is he?" he asked Cortland.

"The doctor says he's a bit better, and I must say he seems to be. As a matter of fact, we just came from the hospital and—"

"The hospital? Is that where he is now?"

"Yes," said Wyatt. "St. Mary's. You didn't know that?"

"How on earth should I know it? When I last spoke to you, he was at home. I asked Dixon to get in touch with his doctor—Thurlow, wasn't it?—and keep me informed on his condition. But since I haven't heard anything, I assumed there was no change."

"It's not a major change, but as young Cortland indicated, it is for the better."

"Well, I couldn't be happier. When I get back from Portsmouth, I'll go see him. I imagine he'll still be there, won't he?"

"I think so. One doesn't get over the effects of as severe a stroke as he had very quickly."

"I know that. Still, if anyone can, it's Cortland. And now, will you excuse me? As I explained, I'm trying to get ready for my trip. And as soon as Dixon gets back with the material I'm waiting for, I'll be off."

"Of course," said Wyatt. There were handshakes, good wishes all around, and they left.

Andrew glanced at Wyatt as they went down the stairs. He was not sure what the point of the visit had been. During their first visit to the Admiralty, Wyatt had told him not to say anything about Reeves and his suspicion that old Mr. Cortland was not suffering from a stroke. This time he had repeated his restrictions to include the mention of curare. But though Wyatt had not seemed to react to anything that was said, and his expression now was quite neutral, Andrew knew him well enough to sense that he had discovered something—something important—and that he was pleased.

"When I asked you before if you had anything planned for this morning," said Wyatt, "you said you didn't have. But you must have had something in mind."

"We did say something to Mrs. Cortland about going boating on the Regent's Park lake," said Andrew. "But Cortland is very interested in the theatre and would very much like to attend a rehearsal, so we thought we'd go there."

"Splendid idea! If you hadn't suggested it, I would."

"Why?"

"Because I have things to do now, but I want to talk to the two of you again later on—and also to Sara and perhaps your mother—and the theatre's a fine, central place to meet."

"All right," said Andrew. "What time shall we expect you?"

Wyatt thought a moment.

"How about five o'clock?"

"Sounds fine. I'll tell mother, and we can have tea together."

"Good. See you then," said Wyatt, and he went striding off along Whitehall toward Scotland Yard.

"I'm afraid I won't be able to be there then," said Cortland.

"Why not?"

"You remember what my stepmother said. That I should be home in time for tea."

"You also heard what the inspector said. That he wants to talk to you again. I think that that should take precedence over what your stepmother said."

"I suppose you're right. What do you think he wants to talk to us about?"

"I don't know, but I have a feeling that it's important. That things are coming to a head."

11

Playing Blind

Andrew and Cortland went east, toward the Strand. It was now almost one o'clock, and they were both hungry; so they went into an oyster shop that had a luncheon bar, and each had a dozen oysters. They arrived at the theatre shortly after Sara and Verna returned from their lunch, but before the rehearsal actually started. This gave Andrew a chance to introduce Cortland to Verna. She had heard about him from Sara as well as Andrew and was very warm and gracious to him, introducing him in turn to Richards, the director, and getting his permission for Cortland as well as Andrew to watch the rehearsal.

The play was coming along nicely, and the rehearsal went smoothly with almost no interruptions. Cortland was impressed with Sara, who played her scenes with great style and had shaded her French accent so that—

while it was still there—you could not miss anything she was saying.

The rehearsal ended at about five, and Andrew took Cortland backstage to Verna's dressing room. She had arranged for tea to be sent in, and they had it there. Andrew was beginning to wonder where Wyatt was when Burke, the watchman, brought Verna a note. She frowned with surprise when she read it, said that there was someone she had to see and asked them to excuse her for a few minutes. They went into the dressing room that Sara shared with two other actresses, just across the corridor from Verna's.

Either because Cortland had been told that his grandfather was better or because Wyatt had become involved in what was happening or both, he was more relaxed and animated than he had been since he and Andrew had come down from school. He asked Sara questions about the play and about the theatre—how the sets were changed, for instance—and she did her best to answer, until suddenly she paused in the middle of a sentence. She glanced at Andrew, but even if she hadn't, he would have known why she hesitated. He had heard someone come down the corridor and go into Verna's dressing room a few minutes before. Now suddenly he heard the voice of the person in there with her, and he knew, as apparently Sara had, that it was Wyatt.

Strange, he thought. Very strange. Why should Wyatt—who was much more their friend than Verna's, and whom Andrew had originally interested in helping Cortland—why should he want to talk privately to Verna? For it was clear now to Andrew now that the note Burke had brought in to her was from Wyatt.

Sara picked up where she had left off, finishing her explanation of how some scenery was lifted up on ropes to the grid overhead and some—the flats—were slid back and stacked in the wings. Cortland nodded and was about to ask her something else when there was a knock at the door.

"Come in if you're fat," said Sara.

The door opened, and Wyatt came in.

"Where did you get that one?" he asked.

"From Burke, the watchman. Why?"

"I just haven't heard it since I went to school. May I sit?"

"Please do."

He pulled a stool from under the dressing counter and sat down.

"We were expecting you for tea," said Andrew. "Too bad you missed it."

"I didn't. Your mother gave me some."

"Oh, good."

At least, Andrew thought, he wasn't making a secret of the fact that he'd been in there talking to her. Wyatt sat for a moment or two, looking at them without saying anything.

"Is anything wrong?" asked Sara finally.

"No. I'm just trying to make up my mind about something."

"About what?" asked Andrew.

"Whether I can trust you or not. And when I say you, I don't mean Cortland as much as I do you and Sara."

"Well, thank you very much!" said Sara indignantly.

"Don't sound so shirty. You know you've given me quite a few problems in the past."

"Maybe we have, but we've also helped you."

"I'll grant you that. You have been helpful several times. As for the problems, you know why they came up? Because every once in a while you became convinced that you're really much cleverer than I am—cleverer than all of Scotland Yard."

"That's not true!" said Sara.

"She means it's not true that we think we're cleverer than anyone else," said Andrew. "But it is true that once or twice we've done things on our own without consulting you about them."

"You admit that?"

"Yes."

"Well, if I involve you in something now, can I trust you to do exactly what I say? But exactly, not going an inch out of the way on your own?"

"Yes, of course," said Sara.

"Do you really think you should answer that quickly? Don't you want to think about it?"

"How can we think about it when we don't know what it's all about?" asked Andrew reasonably. Then, as Wyatt looked at him coldly, "Don't *you* get shirty now. You must know that you can trust us, or you never would have raised this whole thing, whatever it is, in the first place. You just put it the way you did to make us realize it's important. Well, we do. And we'd like to help in any way we can. And we promise to do exactly what you tell us to do, no more and no less. Does that satisfy you?"

"I'm not sure I like your manner, but . . . Yes. I think that satisfies me. Now tell me what you think it's about?"

"That's easy. It's probably about Cortland here. And his grandfather, of course."

"Well, well. A Daniel come to judgment. I never knew so young a body with so old a head."

"You know my methods, Watson, as a certain well-known detective used to say. The question is: Am I right?"

"Of course you are. That brings us to Step Number One. As you probably gathered, I didn't want young Cortland to go home this morning or this afternoon. I still don't—and won't for the foreseeable future. That means I want him to go home with you and stay there, at your house, until I think it's safe for him to leave."

"Well, of course that's fine with me," said Andrew.

"With us," said Sara. "But don't you think we ought to speak to Andrew's mother about it?"

"I already have," said Wyatt. "And she said she'd be delighted to have him stay for as long as I think it necessary."

"That's very kind," said Cortland, a little taken aback. "But I don't have any clothes with me. Shouldn't I go home and get some?"

"Definitely not," said Wyatt. "I've an idea that your stepmother will guess where you are—after all, you did go off with Andrew this morning—and come and try to get you. We'll cover that in Step Two. But, in any case, I don't want you going home. Is that clear?"

"Yes, sir."

"Now for Step Two. As I said, I'm quite sure that someone—Cortland's stepmother or the butler or someone else—will come looking for Cortland. You can handle that in any way you like. You can either deny that he's there or admit that he is and say that he doesn't want to go home and you're not going to make him. But under no circumstances is he to leave. Is that clear, too?"

All three of them nodded, Andrew and Sara noting that Cortland was a little pale and that his eyes were quite large.

"Now we come to Step Number Three—and this is where I don't want any improvisations on your part. This is where I want you to do exactly what I say, so listen carefully. If things start to get sticky—and they very well may—then, no matter when it is, what time of the day or night, you are to come here to the theatre. You are not to go to Scotland Yard or a police station. You are to come here. Is *that* clear?"

"Yes," said Sara. "Only what do you mean by things getting sticky?"

"I mean if things begin to look dangerous or threatening. If, for instance, it looks as if someone may try to break in and take Cortland by force."

"All right," said Sara. "When you say you want us to come here, do you mean all three of us?"

"No, Sara. I want you and Cortland to come here, but I want Andrew to do something else. Do you still have the card that Dixon gave you the first time we went to the Admiralty, Andrew? The one with his home address on it?"

"Yes," said Andrew, taking it out of his pocket. "He told me to give it to Cortland, but I'm afraid I forgot."

"That's all right. Hold on to it. Now, as you know, Sir Arthur's away, but Dixon's here and told you that he's available if you should need him. Well, if things get to a point where you're coming here, then I think it's important that he be here, too. There's no need to say I suggested it. It might be better for everyone concerned if he thought it was all your idea; but go to his house if it's at night and bring him here. Now, any questions?"

They were silent for a moment, looking thoughtfully at one another.

"Yes," said Sara. "Suppose things do get sticky, as you say they might, and we have to do a bunk and come here. Do you want us to do it on the sly, slip away without anyone knowing it, or do you want whoever's around to follow us?"

"A good question, Sara. If you can do it naturally and convincingly—and above all safely—I wouldn't mind having anyone who might be around follow you."

"All right. We'll think of some way of doing it."

"Any other questions?" He glanced at each of them in turn, and, when each had shaken his head, "On your way, then."

Wyatt opened the door, and they followed him out into the corridor. Andrew had been learning a new kind of whist at school called bridge. It was like whist except that at a certain point one of the players laid down his hand, which was then played by his partner. He had a feeling that something similar was taking place here. A game of some sort was going on—a very important one to judge by the tension he felt in Wyatt. But though he, Sara and Cortland were in it, they were not going to be doing the actual playing. They might even, in fact, be *played*.

As he closed the door, the door of Verna's dressing room opened and she came out. She had on her jacket, her hat and gloves and was apparently ready to leave also.

"Hello," she said brightly—a little too brightly, Andrew thought. "Everything settled?"

"I think so," said Andrew. "Peter said you said it was all right for Cortland to come home with us and stay for a while."

"Of course it's all right. We're delighted to have you," she said, smiling at Cortland.

"Thank you very much," he said politely.

Looking at her more closely, Andrew saw that she was trying very hard to appear relaxed and at ease when she wasn't. That meant that, if she wasn't in the game that was being played, she was aware of it.

"Are you going home now, too?" he asked.

"No, dear. I have an engagement. I'm not sure what time I'll be home, but don't worry about it. Fred's taking me and will call for me, so please tell Mrs. Wiggins that I won't be there for dinner. Now how are the three of you going home?"

"Probably take a bus."

"I'd rather you took a cab. Here." She dropped some coins into Andrew's pocket. "Goodbye," she said and hurried up the corridor. They heard her greet someone, then the stage door opened and closed. A moment later Tucker appeared.

"Greetings," he said with an all-inclusive nod. "I won't say good afternoon because I'm not sure it is."

"All right," said Wyatt. "What is it?"

"I gather you've not seen the afternoon papers yet," he said, taking one from his pocket, unfolding it and handing it to him.

Wyatt ran his eye down the first page, paused at the bottom and swore softly to himself.

"What is it?" asked Sara.

"We had another neat little bit of dipping last night," said Tucker. "That's pickpocketing," he explained to Cortland. "The bloke that was dipped was a French banker with plenty in his purse. At least, so he claimed when he reported it at the police station. He was mad as a wet hen, according to the sergeant, claiming that something like that could never happen in Paris. And what's he done but say the same thing to the press. What we need, according to him, is to have the French Sûreté come over here and teach us how to catch our thieves."

"The commissioner's going to like that," said Andrew.

"Not half, he will!"

"Yes, we really needed that," said Wyatt. "Still . . ." He shrugged, then looked at the three young people. "You've got your instructions," he said. "Off you go."

They went on up the corridor, said goodnight to Burke, pushed open the heavy iron door and went out into the alley. As they started up it toward the Strand, they heard the brassy strains of a street band playing "From Greenland's Icy Mountains."

"What's that?" asked Cortland.

"Hurry up and you'll see," said Sara.

They walked more quickly and reached the Strand just as the Samaritan band went by: the two thin men and one lady blowing their horns, the intense lady shaking her tambourine and the plump and jolly man pounding the big bass drum with unflagging enthusiasm. The dirty-faced urchins still accompanied them, running in and out of the crowds on the pavement. And the neat, well-scrubbed boy with the carefully brushed hair walked alongside them, making clear by his manner that he was with the uniformed players, the saved and the godly, and had nothing to do with the unkempt ragamuffins.

"Who are they?" asked Cortland.

"Samaritans," said Sara. "They're like the Salvation Army. They collect money to help feed and buy clothes for the poor."

"Do they come around here often?"

"Almost every night. They probably collect more tin around here than anywhere else. People are easy with it when they're going to theatre and such."

Cortland nodded.

Alf and Liz, the pearly buskers, were just arriving for their evening performance for the theatre queue further up the street, and Andrew waved to them. They waved back, Alf touching his cap and Liz dropping him a mock curtsey.

A four-wheeler was coming up the Strand, and Andrew ran out to hail it and brought it over for Sara and Cortland to get into. He told the cabby where they wanted to go, got in himself and off they went to St. John's Wood.

12

The Watchers in the Dark

Matson let them in and bowed gravely when he was told that Cortland would be staying with them for a few days. Mrs. Wiggins was, as usual, more responsive. She told Cortland that she had heard about him from Sara and Andrew, was delighted that he was going to be staying with them and insisted on taking him upstairs and showing him his room. When they came down, Andrew remembered to tell her that his mother would not be home for dinner.

"That's all right," said Mrs. Wiggins. "We're as used to that as we are to unexpected guests. The thing is, would you mind very much if we had dinner just a bit on the early side? It's Mr. Matson's choir night."

Along with several other surprising qualities, Matson had an extremely good voice and sang with the local choir. Andrew said of course they wouldn't mind. That they'd had quite a big day and would be glad, not only to eat a bit earlier than usual, but to get to bed early.

Dinner was as good as it always was. Cortland was particularly impressed with Mrs. Simmond's fruit tart, one of her specialties. They were all in the parlor playing parcheesi when Matson tapped tentatively at the door.

"Will you be requiring anything further, Master Andrew?" he asked.

"No, Matson. I gather you're off to church."

"If you've no objection."

"Of course not."

"Sing well, Matson," said Sara. "We'll be there to listen to you on Sunday."

"I'll do my best, Miss Sara, tonight and Sunday."

He bowed and was about to go upstairs and get his coat and hat when there was a loud knock on the front door.

"I'll get it," said Andrew.

"No, Master Andrew. I have plenty of time."

He went to the door in his usual, unhurried way and opened it—not as wide as he did when guests were expected—but only partway. Still he had opened it sufficiently for Andrew to see who had knocked. It was Hodge, the Cortland's butler.

"Evening," he said, in his rasping voice. "I'm Mrs. Benedict Cortland's man. Is young Cortland here?"

"I will inquire," said Matson smoothly.

"What do you mean, you'll inquire? You'd know if he was here or if he wasn't, wouldn't you?"

"I said I will inquire," said Matson without changing his expression or raising his voice, and he slammed the door in Hodge's face.

"We heard," said Andrew when Matson turned around, for by now Sara and young Cortland had joined him out in the entrance hall.

"What are we going to do?" whispered Cortland. "The inspector said he didn't want me to go home. That he wanted me to stay here."

"And so you shall," said Andrew. "Say that he is here, but he's going to stay, Matson."

"Very well, Master Andrew." He went to the door as sedately as he had before, but this time, before he opened it, he slid the chain that secured it into its catch so that it only opened about eight or ten inches.

"Well?" Hodge's battered face was thrust aggressively close to the opening in the door.

"Young Master Cortland is here."

"We thought he was. All right. Send him out. I'm to take him home."

"I'm sorry, but he does not wish to go home. He prefers to remain here."

"He what?"

"I said, he prefers to remain here."

"Why, the young scut! You send him out here and be sharp about it, or it'll be the worse for you!"

"Indeed?"

"Don't you try to come it over me with those lah-de-dah manners! I know all about butling! But that ain't all I know. If you opened that door and came out here, I'd bash you proper, I would! Now you send young Cortland out here to me, or I'm going to the police!"

"That is a perfectly splendid idea. It will save me the necessity of sending the coachman there. The police station is on the Wellington Road, and the sergeant's name is Doggett. He's a good friend of mine, so give him my regards. Good night." And with sudden forcefulness he slammed and locked the door.

"Well done, Matson," said Andrew. "Very well done indeed."

"Thank you, Master Andrew." Then, as Hodge began a furious tattoo, alternately kicking the door and using the knocker, "Shall I stop at the police station and tell them about this? It's not out of my way."

"I don't think that's really necessary. But be careful when you leave. As you've probably gathered, he's quite a violent fellow."

"He doesn't frighten me, Master Andrew. However, I'd like to say that I can easily miss choir practice. I mean, if you thought it would be helpful if I stayed here . . ."

"I don't, Matson. We'll be fine. You go ahead."

"Well, if you're following instructions from Inspector Wyatt as Master Cortland suggested, then I'm sure you'll be all right." And bowing, he went upstairs to get his things as he had started to do when Hodge had knocked.

He came down a few minutes later, his bowler set squarely on his head, umbrella under his arm, pulling on his gloves.

"I'll let you out and lock up after you, Matson," said Andrew.

"I was going to suggest that, Master Andrew. Lock and bolt the door. I have the key to the back door, and I'll come in that way."

"Very good, Matson." He opened the door, and Matson went out and stood there for a moment on the top step, looking around and then up at the overcast sky, as if to see whether he should put up his umbrella.

"Can you hear me, Master Andrew?" he said very quietly without turning around.

"Yes, Matson."

"There's a carriage up the street near the entrance to Three Oaks. Our violent friend is talking to someone in it, and it looks to me as if he's planning to remain here for a while. Are you still sure you don't want me to stay home this evening?"

Andrew hesitated a moment. Evidently Wyatt had anticipated something like this, which was why he had given them such strict instructions. On the other hand, Andrew did not consider that things—to use Wyatt's phrase—had gotten really sticky yet.

"Thank you, Matson, but I still don't think there's any need to do that."

"Very well. However, I think I should tell you that Fred is back, and I took the liberty of sending a note over to the stable telling him to stand by until I got home."

"You seem to have thought of everything, Matson. Thank you again, and I'm sure we'll be fine until you get home."

Matson bowed, went down the steps, across the front garden and turned right on Rysdale Road, away from Hodge and the carriage, on his way to the church.

Andrew locked and bolted the door, went back into the sitting room and told Sara and Cortland what Matson had said.

"Why does Hodge—or rather my stepmother—want me so badly?" asked Cortland. "She doesn't care that much about me. In fact, she doesn't like me at all. She's always happy to have me go back to school."

"It's because of your grandfather," said Sara. "Because she thinks she can use you to get hold of him again or use you to get him to do something she wants."

"I still don't really understand it, but I think you're right. She was never the least bit interested in me till he came back to England from Germany. But if that's the case—I mean that it's me that she wants—perhaps I should go. Otherwise it might become dangerous for the two of you."

"Don't you even think of going!" said Sara fiercely.

"Peter Wyatt said that you were to stay with us, and that's what you're going to do."

"Sara's right," said Andrew. "He told us what he wanted us to do, and that's what we should do. Meanwhile, how about another game of Parcheesi?"

They played several more games, played until Cortland began yawning, and looking at his watch, Andrew saw that it was almost ten o'clock. He suggested that it was time they went up to bed, and Sara and Cortland agreed. They had folded the board, put the dice and counters into their box, when Cortland suddenly became very still.

"What is it?" asked Sara, unconsciously dropping her voice.

"I'm not absolutely sure," said Cortland, "but I thought I saw someone out there in the garden."

"Where?" asked Andrew, who had his back to the French doors.

"Over near the bushes."

Sara and Andrew looked at one another.

"We're all a little nervy," said Sara. "He could have imagined it."

"He could. On the other hand, he might be right." He stood up. "You two open the board up and start another game."

"What are you going to do?" asked Cortland.

"There's another back door beside the kitchen door. It opens off the larder, and you can't really see it from the outside. I'm going out that way. I'll do an Indian stalk through the garden and see if there really is anyone out there."

"All right," said Sara. "But be careful."

"I will. But I don't have too much to worry about. It's Cortland they want, not me."

He strolled casually out of the sitting room without looking at the window, went through the dining room, the pantry, the kitchen and into the larder without striking a match. He had to move carefully through the larder, for it was quite full of things, and at one point he almost knocked over a flour barrel; but he finally reached the door, eased the bolt back and opened it very quietly.

He remained there for a moment, listening and peering out into the darkness. It was a very dark night. It had become grey late in the afternoon, and now clouds completely hid the moon and stars. The night air was fresh and laced with some of the first smells of spring; the heady scent of early roses, of the laburnum and rhododendron and the sweet smell of apple and chestnut blossoms from the large estate of Three Oaks next door.

Andrew started around the back of the house, moving slowly and quietly. The only light in sight at this point was in Fred's room over the stables. That meant Fred had obeyed Matson's instructions and was still up, which was good.

He was on the west side of the house now, the side

with the sitting room windows. Crouching as he went past the kitchen windows, he glanced to his right and froze. Ahead were the bushes where Cortland thought he had seen someone. They were between Andrew and the far-off glow of a streetlight on Rysdale Road. And distant as that light was, it provided enough illumination for him to see, not one, but two shapes hiding in the bushes!

He closed his eyes, tried to make himself relax. Were there really two figures there or was he imagining it? He tried to recall exactly what the bushes were, how they were shaped. Two of them were rose bushes, but the one in the center was a rhododendron; it was near it that he thought he had seen the figures. Why there? Because roses have thorns, idiot, and if someone is going to hide in the bushes, they would choose to do it in a rhododendron rather than a rose bush. He opened his eyes and looked again. The figures were still there. And they seemed to have moved a little. Did he dare go any closer to make absolutely certain, see if he could recognize them? No. But what if he went completely around the house and approached them from the street side? If he did that, coming up behind them, he could see them silhouetted against the light in the living room. It was worth trying.

He turned and went back around the rear of the house, still moving carefully. He was halfway down the east side of the house now, keeping close to it, when he froze again—not because of anything he saw, but because of what he heard: a faint, muffled cough. Crouching, he looked to his right. And there, standing behind a hawthorn, he saw a third figure—not only saw it, but saw it move. For after the cough, the man reached up to pull his muffler closer about his neck.

He was convinced now that he had not imagined the two near the rose bushes. So there were at least three of them standing outside the house, watching it. Was that all they were going to do, watch it? Or, at some point, were they going to try to break in? There was, of course, no way of telling. But it seemed to Andrew that the situation had now become what Wyatt had characterized as sticky.

Moving as quietly, but more quickly than he had before, he went back along the side of the house and in through the larder door. He closed and bolted it, then went back through the kitchen, the pantry and the dining room to the sitting room.

Sara and Cortland were where he had left them, sitting at the table in front of the window, pretending to be playing still another game of Parcheesi.

"Well?" said Sara.

"He didn't imagine it. There are two men over there, near the bushes, and one on the other side of the house over near the Three Oaks wall."

"Three of them?"

"Yes. At least three. And Hodge further up the street."

"What are we going to do?" asked Cortland in a hushed, rather anxious voice.

"You know. The inspector told us what to do."

"Go to the theatre."

"Yes. I don't know what the men are planning to do, whether they'd dare break in here, but I think we should go as soon as we can. What I don't know is how we're going to manage it—how we're going to get out of here without having them get hold of Cortland. . . ."

"I know how," said Sara. "I thought of a way some time ago."

"How?"

"Never mind how. Do you trust me, Benedict?" she asked Cortland, calling him by his first name for the first time. "Will you do just as I say?"

"Yes, Sara."

"All right, then. Go get Fred," she said to Andrew. "Go out the front door and walk back to the stable the way you would if nothing were wrong. In other words, you haven't any idea that anyone is out there. Have Fred bring the carriage around here, and Bendict and I will be ready." Then, as he hesitated, "What's wrong? Benedict hardly knows me, and he trusts me. Why are you acting as if you don't?"

"I'm sorry. I didn't mean to. It's just . . . All right. I'm going."

He unchained and unlocked the door and went out. He stood for a moment just where Matson had stood, looking out toward Rysdale Road. Just beyond the hedge to the left, he could make out a dark shape that was probably Hodge. And further to the left, near the wall around Three Oaks, he could see the carriage Matson had mentioned. He went down the steps, out from under the porte cochere and around the house to the stable, carefully avoiding looking at the bushes where he had seen the two men lurking.

The light was still on in Fred's room, and the carriage was out in front of the stable, which meant that Fred intended to call for Verna somewhere. But the horses were inside for, like a good coachman, Fred had unhitched them when he got home, undoubtedly rubbed them down and put them into their stalls for a feed until they were needed again.

By the time Andrew had slid open the stable door, Fred—who must have heard him—was coming down the stairs.

"What's up?" he asked.

"We need the carriage, Fred."

"I thought you might, and I've been waiting since I got Matson's note. In a hurry, are you?"

"A bit."

"Then you'd better help with the horses. You take Jack out, while I get Jerry." He went into the first stall, untied the bay gelding and backed him out. "Is this one of the inspector's dos?"

"Yes."

"I thought that, too. Better get cracking." He went into the second stall to get the other horse while Andrew led Jack out, backed him into place and began to hitch him up. Fred came out with Jerry, and in less than ten minutes the carriage was ready to go.

"Now what?" said Fred, climbing up into the box.

"Around front to pick up Sara and a friend of mine," said Andrew climbing up beside him. "Sara will tell you where to go?"

"What about you?"

"I'm going somewhere else."

"Like that, eh? All right."

He shook the reins, drove the carriage around the house and under the porte cochere.

"They should be ready. I'll get them," said Andrew, jumping down from the box. As he ran up the steps, the door opened, and Andrew paused in midstride. Sara had lit the gaslights in the entrance hall, and it was now as bright as day. Standing there beside Sara, and clearly visible at least as far away as the street, was another girl just an inch or so taller than Sara. It was only when Andrew recognized the girl's dress and bonnet as Sara's that he realized what she had done—that she had disguised Cortland by dressing him as a girl.

"I'm going to take Meg home," she said in a clear, carrying voice. "But there's no need for you to come too unless you want to."

"No, I think I'll stay here with Cortland," he said,

understanding now how she planned to get Cortland out of the house and away without running the risk of having him captured. "Don't forget that you want to be followed," he said under his breath.

"I know that," she said in the same way. Then aloud, "Come on, Meg."

They went down the steps, Andrew opened the carriage door, and they got in.

"Where to?" asked Fred.

"The theatre," said Sara from inside the carriage. "Start out slowly. Then, when I tell you, you can get cracking."

"Yes, m'lady," said Fred, who may not have known what was going on, but was nevertheless enjoying the situation. He shook the reins, sent the carriage down the driveway and left on Rysdale Road.

Sara had carefully placed Cortland next to the left hand window. As they made the turn into Rysdale Road, she glanced past him and saw that Matson had been right. Hodge was standing near the curb. He had been watching the house, but now he was studying the carriage with a puzzled frown. As they passed him and the yellow glow of a streetlight was full on the window, Sara adroitly knocked off Cortland's bonnet, revealing his face. Hodge started, stared, then went running down the street toward the carriage that was waiting near the entrance to Three Oaks.

"All right, Fred," called Sara. "Now go!"

Cracking his whip, Fred put the horses into a fast trot. As they went past the waiting carriage, Cortland said, "Why, that's Dr. Thurlow's carriage!"

"Who's he?"

"The doctor who was taking care of my grandfather. And a friend of my stepmother's."

"The yobbo that was acting as crow got in the brougham," said Fred," and it's following us. Want me to give 'em the slip?"

"No, Fred," said Sara. "Act as if you're trying to—pull away a bit—but let them keep us in sight."

"Hoicks, yoicks and tally-ho," said Fred. Again he cracked his whip, but at the same time he kept a slight pressure on the reins to keep the horses at the same pace.

The brougham was about two hundred yards behind them when they reached Prince Albert Road, and Fred kept them at that distance as they went south on Park Road and continued working his way south and east toward the Strand. They came down Regent Street and the Haymarket, and when they reached Trafalgar Square, Sara said, "All right, Fred. Now give us as much of a lead as you can."

Again Fred cracked his whip over the horses' heads, but this time he shook out the reins and they went into an even faster trot. There was not much traffic on the Strand, and Fred worked his way skillfully through what there was. By the time he drew up in front of the theatre, he had gained another hundred yards on their pursuers.

"Good work, Fred. Thanks!" said Sara, opening the carriage door and jumping out. "Come on, Benedict." And taking him by the hand, she led him at a dead run up the alley toward the stage door.

It was only then that it occurred to her that Burke, the watchman, might not be there. What would they do then? Where could they go? For she knew that in a minute or so, Hodge and whoever was in the carriage would be coming up the alley after them. She pounded on the heavy stage door, meanwhile looking back up the alley toward the Strand. When there was no answer, she tried the door. It wasn't locked. She pulled it open, hurried in and closed it behind Cortland. A gaslight was burning in the corridor outside Burke's cubbyhole, but he wasn't there.

"What do we do now?" asked Cortland.

This was something else they hadn't discussed, and Sara hadn't really thought about.

"I don't know. I guess hide until Andrew gets here."

"Where can we hide?"

"On the far side of the stage where the flats are stored. Come on."

And she led him down the corridor and across the large, dark, empty stage.

Standing under the porte cochere, Andrew watched Fred go left on Rysdale Road past Hodge, saw Hodge run over to the waiting brougham and climb up onto the box and then saw the brougham make a sweeping turn and begin chasing the Tillett's carriage. Then he ran across the garden, turned right and hurried up the street.

There was a cab stand near the pub on the corner of Wellington Road, and he hoped he would find a cab there. He was in luck. A hansom was just drawing up when he got there. He jumped in and, taking out Mr. Dixon's card, gave the cabby his address, which was on Woburn Square in Bloomsbury, and told him there'd be an extra shilling for him if he hurried. Delighted at the idea, the cabby turned the hansom, cracked his whip and went bowling down Wellington Road.

At that hour there was even less traffic in that part of London than in the theatre district, and they made very good time. The address that Mr. Dixon had given him proved to be a dignified stucco house. Telling the cab to wait, Andrew jumped out, ran up the steps and rapped sharply with the knocker. A moment or two later a woman's voice asked who was there.

"I have an urgent message for Mr. Dixon," he said.

Apparently this was not an unusual occurrence, for the door was immediately unlocked and opened. A middle-aged woman in a wrapper and cap, apparently his housekeeper, stood there.

"I believe he's still up," she said. "If you'll wait a minute, I'll see."

A door behind her opened.

"I am up, Mrs. Hunter," said Dixon. Then, looking at

Andrew, "You're young Tillett, Cortland's friend, aren't you?"

"Yes, sir. I met you when I came to the Admiralty with Inspector Wyatt. You gave me your card and told me that if Cortland ever needed you . . ."

"I remember. Come in." He ushered Andrew into a large and comfortable study and closed the door. "I was doing some work," he said, nodding toward a desk that was covered with papers, "when I heard your knock. Now what's this all about?"

"It's about Cortland, sir. I'm afraid he's in danger."

"What sort of danger?"

It wasn't going to be easy to tell a coherent story while keeping Wyatt's name and role out of it, but Andrew did the best he could. He told about the fire at the Cortland house and the fact that Cortland's grandfather had been taken to St. Mary's Hospital without mentioning Beasley's participation either.

"Cortland found this very upsetting," he said, "and this morning he asked if he couldn't come and stay with me rather than go home."

"Why did he want to do that? What was he afraid of?"

"I believe of his stepmother, who—he seemed to think—had had something to do with what had happened to his grandfather. I said of course and took him home with me."

He went on to describe what had happened that evening; Hodge's appearance and attempt to get Cortland to come home with him, his threats, his waiting outside in the street and finally about the other men Andrew had seen lurking outside in the bushes.

Dixon, sitting on the edge of his desk, listened quietly and intently to everything Andrew said, his eyes never leaving his face.

"Who were these other men?" he asked.

"I don't know, sir. I assumed that they had something to do with Hodge."

"What did you do?"

"My mother and our butler were both out, and I was afraid that Hodge and the other men might try to break into the house to get hold of Cortland, so my friend Sara Wiggins and I smuggled him out of the house and she took him off to the Windsor Theatre."

"Why did you do that? Why didn't you get in touch with Inspector Wyatt?"

"Because we didn't know where he was," said Andrew—which was certainly true as far as it went. "And we're familiar with the theatre because my mother's been rehearsing there, and Sara's in the play too, and we knew it would be empty now and thought it would be a good place for Cortland to hide. The thing is, I'm afraid that Hodge and whoever was with him may have followed them."

"I see," said Dixon. "In that case, I think we'd better do something about it."

"You mean, you'll come there with me?"

"Of course."

"I hoped you might. I came here in a hansom, and I told him to wait."

"Well, well," said Dixon approvingly. "I can see why Inspector Wyatt seemed so interested in what you had to say. You've behaved with an intelligence far beyond your years throughout."

"Thank you, sir."

Though he did not say so, it occurred to Andrew that he was having an opportunity to see why Sir Arthur had talked so glowingly about his secretary. For, having asked a minimum of questions and having made up his mind, Dixon moved with smooth efficiency and without a wasted motion. He took off his velvet smoking jacket, put on his frock coat and top hat. He paused for a moment in front of the umbrella stand in the corner, started to take out an umbrella, but instead plucked out a sturdy, silver-handled cane, which he tucked under his arm.

"After you," he said to Andrew, opening the door for him.

13

The Curtain Falls

Mr. Dixon was silent during the ride from Woburn Square to the Strand, staring straight ahead with his crossed hands resting on the head of his cane. Respecting his mood and the gravity of the situation, Andrew did not say anything either, though he did glance occasionally at the stern face of his companion.

Dixon roused himself when the hansom drew up in front of the theatre, got out and paid the cabby—giving him a handsome tip to judge by the cabby's thanks. Then, turning to Andrew, "How do we get in?" he asked.

"This way," said Andrew, leading him down the alley.

He knocked on the metal stage door as Sara had done a short while before and, when there was no response, tried it, found it open and went in followed by Dixon.

"Isn't there a watchman here?" asked Dixon.

"There is usually. In there," said Andrew, nodding toward Burke's cubbyhole. "But he's either making his rounds, looking over the theatre, or else he's slipped out for a few minutes to get something to eat."

"If he was making his rounds, going through the theatre, wouldn't he need that?" asked Dixon indicating a bull's-eye lantern that stood on a shelf in the cubbyhole.

"Yes, he would. It's dark in the theatre. That means he's gone out."

"Yes. I'm sure he won't mind if I borrow this," said Dixon, striking a match and lighting the lantern. Then, picking it up, "As I'm sure you've gathered, this is a very serious matter we have here, and there's not much time, so I'll be brief. Can I rely on you to do exactly what you're told?"

"Of course."

"Then I want you to leave here immediately and go home. Don't worry about your friend, Cortland, or the girl. I'll take care of them, and I'll be in touch with you later this evening. In the meantime, you're not to talk to anyone about any of this. Is that clear?"

"Yes, sir."

"Off you go, then."

Andrew walked back to the stage door, opened it and looked over his shoulder. Dixon had his back to him and was looking down the corridor toward the stage. Slamming the door as if he had gone out, Andrew slipped into the open closet, next to Burke's cubbyhole, in which the stagehands and other theatre workers usually kept their coats. There were some aprons and coveralls hanging there now, and he hid behind them. Dixon might be with the Admiralty, but he wasn't Wyatt. And though Andrew meant it when he said he could be relied on to do what he was told, it depended on who did the telling. In this case, he wasn't about to go off and leave Sara and Cortland to the care of Dixon, no matter how efficient the man might be.

A moment later he was glad he had done what he did, for Dixon came to the stage door and bolted it on the inside, which meant that neither Burke nor anyone else would be able to come in that way. Then, directing the beam of the bull's-eye lantern ahead of him, he started down the corridor toward the stage.

Andrew waited till Dixon was well along the corridor, past the single gaslight that burned high on the wall, then followed.

Something was wrong, very wrong. Why had Dixon locked the outside door? Where were Sara and Cortland? And where were Hodge and whoever had been with him when he followed Sara and Cortland?

Moving quietly along the corridor, Andrew was acutely aware of the huge, dark, quiet theatre. The still air smelled of dust, paint, glue sizing and greasepaint. Dixon's footsteps, which he made no attempt to muffle, sounded loud in the heavy silence, and high up overhead in the grid where old backcloths hung, a draft shook one of the dozens of ropes that ran up there so that it tapped insistently against the canvas.

Dixon paused in the centre of the dark stage, slowly swinging the beam of his lantern over the backstage area and over the wings opposite him.

"All right," he said. "Where are you?"

Andrew was now in the right-hand wings, standing near the base of the proscenium arch. Beyond the unlit footlights he could just make out the shape of the auditorium, the curve of the balcony and the gilt scallops of the boxes.

"I said, where are you?" repeated Dixon. "Didn't you hear me, Helga, Thurlow?"

"Who is it?" asked an uncertain female voice.

"Who do you think it is?"

There was the sound of footsteps, and Cortland's stepmother and Dr. Thurlow appeared from behind some furniture that had been piled up backstage and came toward him.

"How did you know we were here?" asked Dr. Thurlow.

"What difference does it make? Where's young Cortland?"

"He's here somewhere," said Mrs. Cortland. "He was staying at the house of his friend in St. John's Wood. We sent Hodge to get him, but he wouldn't come. Later he sneaked out with a young girl and came here. We were just looking for him when we heard you come in."

"And where's Hodge?"

"Outside in the alley," said Thurlow. "He'll catch Cortland if he tries to get out that way, and he'll warn us if the watchman or anyone else is coming in."

"No, he won't. I locked the stagedoor."

Mrs. Cortland and Thurlow were close to him now. "I suppose you're armed?" he said to Thurlow.

"Yes."

"You would be. Give me the gun."

"What?"

"I said, give me the gun."

He spoke quietly, but with so much authority that Thurlow could not oppose him. He took a revolver from his pocket and handed it to Dixon.

"Thank you." Dixon thrust it into the waistband of his trousers, set the bulls-eye lantern on the table the prompter used during rehearsals and stood there for a moment, leaning on his cane. "You fools!" he said suddenly, his voice icy with contempt. "You ridiculous, blundering fools!"

"Please," said Mrs. Cortland, her accent more pronounced than it had ever been before. "You must not blame us. You approved the plan. And just because the boy got away from us for a while . . ."

"He did not just get away. He may have brought Scotland Yard into the affair. I said you were fools. You are worse than fools, for you have undone the work of years, made it impossible for me to continue where I am. And for that there is only one answer."

Twisting the silver handle of the cane, he pulled out the long slim swordblade it contained and, with a fencer's lunge, stabbed Thurlow in the chest. Thurlow stood there for a moment, looking at him in astonishment, then his knees buckled, and he fell face down on the stage. Even as he fell, Dixon pulled out the blade and lunged again. This time Mrs. Cortland staggered back, tried to turn and flee, then collapsed and fell, looking upward with sightless eyes.

"Drop that blade, Dixon!" said a voice from the darkened auditorium.

"What? Who's that?"

"That's not a serious question. You must know."

"Wyatt. So this was a trap!"

"It was. I have men outside in the street, in the alley, out in back and here in the theatre. Which leads me to ask: How in the name of sanity did you expect to kill two people and get away with it?"

"I did not have much choice," said Dixon calmly. "As for getting away, I still plan to do so." With movements as swift and sure as when he had assassinated the two who lay on the stage, he picked up the lantern, directed its beam into the wings opposite Andrew and at the same time pulled out and leveled the revolver.

"Cortland, you and the girl with you, come out here!"

Looking past him, Andrew's heart skipped a beat, and he went cold with fear. For the lantern's beam picked out Sara and Cortland crouching down between two stacks of flats. Andrew didn't know whether they had been there all the time or had started to come out when they heard Wyatt's voice, but Dixon had either seen them or heard them moving, and now he had them pinned there with the lantern's beam.

"I said: Come out!" said Dixon, his voice sharper and more menacing. "Come out, or I'll shoot!"

"Sara! Cortland, do as he says!" said Wyatt, trying to keep his voice level.

As Sara and Cortland stood up and came slowly out of the wings toward the stage, Andrew heard a faint noise behind him. Turning, he saw Burke standing near the rack to which all the overhead ropes were tied. If he had ever looked old, ill or ineffectual, he did not look that way now, and Andrew suddenly realized that of course he must be a policeman, too.

"What are you up to, Dixon?" asked Wyatt, coming forward in the dark auditoriums so that he was just visible at the edge of the lantern light.

"I'm sure you can guess," said Dixon, putting the lantern down in the prompter's table again, but holding the gun steadily on Sara and Cortland. "First of all, you must recognize the fact that I have nothing to lose. I have already killed two people, so I would have absolutely no hesitation about killing these two youngsters here."

"What are you leading up to?"

"Isn't that obvious? I want a safe-conduct to a German ship, the *Leipzig*, now at St. Katherine's Docks. These two shall come with me. If all goes well, when we are out at sea and drop the pilot, I will release them to return here with him. But if you make a false move, attempt to capture me, I shall kill them."

"You wouldn't dare!"

"My dear Inspector, you can only hang me once no matter what I do from now on!"

Andrew caught another movement out of the corner of his eye, turned and saw the flash of a knife as Burke cut something, looked at Andrew, looked up and then looked at Dixon. In that moment Andrew knew what Burke was trying to do and what he—Andrew—must do. Stepping away from the proscenium so that he would be silhouetted against the glow of the gaslight further up the corridor, he raised a hand to attract Sara's attention. She saw him, glanced at Dixon whose back was to Andrew, then looked at Andrew again. He put his fingers to his lips in warning, then motioned toward the footlights. Sara may not have known why he wanted her to do it, but such was her faith in Andrew that, taking Cortland's arm, she began to edge downstage toward the footlights.

"Well?" said Dixon.

"I haven't the authority to give you a safe-conduct," said Wyatt. "I can't just let a murderer and spy go."

"If you haven't the authority, you'd better take it!" said Dixon. "Would it make it any easier for you if I killed one of these two children now to prove I'm capable of it? That would still leave one to take with me as a hostage."

"No!" said Wyatt. He hesitated, his face strained. "Will you give me time to talk to the Home Secretary about it? I'm sure he'll agree, but . . ."

"I will not," said Dixon. "You'll give me your answer now—right now." Though his gun had continued to point at Sara and Cortland, following them as they edged slowly, almost imperceptibly downstage toward the footlights, he now realized for the first time that they had changed position. "What are you doing?" he asked sharply. "Where do you think you're going?"

"Nowhere," said Sara with wide-eyed and deceptive meekness,

"Well then, stand still!" They were well downstage now, almost at the footlights, and as a result, the gun was pointed almost directly into the auditorium. "No, I think you'd better come back here. Did you hear me? Come back here, or—"

Burke had been loosening one particular rope, holding it with a single turn around the rack; now he released it, and the heavy curtain, without the sandbags that counterbalanced it, came crashing down like a guillotine. It just missed Dixon's head, but hit his extended arm and broke it like a dry stick. He staggered back with a strangled cry, the gun dropping from his helpless hand, and sank to one knee, clutching his broken arm. Before he could move again, even think of trying to pick up the gun with his left hand, Burke was upon him. He kicked the gun across the stage and snapped a pair of handcuffs on him.

Though the lowered curtain cut off Andrew's view of the auditorium and of Sara and Cortland, he could hear excited voices, queries and answers, on the far side of it. There were running footsteps, the pass door in the proscenium arch was thrown open, and Wyatt and Tucker, followed by Sara and Cortland, came in to join Burke and Andrew backstage.

"Well done, Burke," said Wyatt after a quick glance at the moaning, handcuffed Dixon. "I thought you might be up to something like this. That's why I kept him talking."

"Young Andrew was the one who really did it," said Burke. "I cut the sandbags loose, but he was the one who got Miss Sara and Cortland to move downstage so I could drop the curtain where it would do the most good."

"Are they both dead?" asked Cortland, staring down at his stepmother and Thurlow with fascinated horror.

"I'm afraid so," said Tucker, who had been examining

them. "Wait a minute! She is, but the doctor's still breathing!"

"Lung," whispered Thurlow. "Get me to hospital."

Hurrying to the pass door, Wyatt called the constables who had been in the auditorium, had them come backstage and gave them rapid instructions. Thurlow and Dixon were to be taken to the nearest hospital—the French Hospital on Shaftesbury Avenue—where they could be treated; but they were to be kept under heavy guard around the clock. He made Burke responsible for them, and under Burke's orders, Dixon was immediately helped out and Thurlow carried out on a stretcher.

"What about her?" asked Sara quietly, looking at Mrs. Cortland.

"Can't move her till the police surgeon's looked at her," said Wyatt. But he had Tucker cover her with a blanket and led the three young people off the stage and into Verna's dressing room, which was the largest of them.

"I have a lot to do," he said, sitting on the dressing table. "But I suspect you have some questions, and I feel I owe it to you to answer them."

"We certainly do have questions," said Sara. But before she could begin to ask them, the stage door opened, there were quick footsteps, and Verna came in.

"Fred came to get me," she said a little breathlessly. "He said he'd brought Sara and young Cortland here, and . . ." She glanced at the two of them and at Andrew. "Is everyone all right?"

"You can see that they are," said Wyatt. "It's all over. And very satisfactorily so."

"Oh," said Verna, visibly relaxing. "I'm glad. In spite of everything you said, all your assurances, I was worried. But now I'd like you to tell me all the things that you didn't tell me before."

"I was just about to do so," said Wyatt. "I'm sure you understand a good deal of the story already," he said to Cortland. "But I'll begin at the beginning anyway. Did Andrew tell you what Sir Arthur Barry had to say about your father when we first went to the Admiralty?" Cortland nodded. "Good. He admired him very much, thought he was a very good, very intelligent and courageous officer, and it was he who got him the appointment of naval attaché, first in Copenhagen and then in Berlin. Your father's outspoken opposition to the Heligoland agreement made the Germans decide to keep an eye on him, and they must have become aware of it very quickly when he began to suspect that there was an intelligence leak somewhere, possibly in the Admiralty itself."

"A spy?" said Sara.

"Let's say an enemy agent, by which I mean someone working for another country. In this case, Germany. I don't know what evidence Captain Cortland dug up—

and we probably never will know—but it must have been quite important and quite convincing, for when he went on his holiday to the Baltic, someone saw to it that he did not come back."

"In other words, you think he was murdered," said Andrew.

"I'm fairly certain of it," said Wyatt.

"It never occurred to me that it was anything but an accident," said Cortland. "But I think it did to my grandfather."

"It certainly did," said Wyatt. "He'd had dealings with the Germans in Africa and was just as suspicious of them as your father had been. When he returned here, he went to see Sir Arthur at the Admiralty, questioned him and then went to Germany to see what he could find out there."

"And did he find out anything?" asked Cortland.

"Yes and no. As you know, the case has been solved—and principally as a result of his efforts—but not in a conventional way. He didn't come up with any concrete proof that your father had been murdered, but he was more convinced than ever that he had been and that the reason for it was the one I gave you: he had found evidence of an enemy agent in very high places. So he did something very ingenious."

"This is Cortland's grandfather you're talking about?" said Verna, who had been listening with great interest. "The one who's now at St. Mary's Hospital?"

"Yes."

"What did he do?" asked Sara.

"He sent telegrams to his son's widow and to Sir Arthur at the Admiralty saying he'd made some very interesting discoveries that he'd tell them about when he came back."

"And had he made any discoveries?" asked Cortland.

"No. What he was doing was preparing a trap. And the bait was an old and rather battered dispatch box that he got from a friend of your father's at the embassy in Berlin. He knew he was being watched by the German secret police, so he kept the box with him, guarding it every minute during his trip home. The impression that he wanted to give—and apparently did give—was that it contained the evidence for which your father had been killed, proof of the identity of the enemy agent at the Admiralty."

"What happened to the box?" asked Andrew.

"That was what several people wondered. He had it with him when he got on the boat in Germany. He had it with him when he got on the train from Harwich to London. But he didn't have it when he got to his daughter-in-law's house on Sherburne Square."

"He hid it somewhere on his way from the station!" said Sara.

"Actually, he destroyed it, flattened it and threw it out of the train window just before he reached London."

"But why?" asked Cortland.

"I know!" said Andrew. "Because he wanted people to think that he *had* hidden it somewhere!"

"Exactly. It was *his* security, *his* safe conduct. He had no illusions about who or what he was up against, knew that they would kill him with no more compunction than they had his son. But they did not dare do that until they had gotten hold of the dispatch box, which they thought contained vital evidence. On the other hand, they were afraid he might give them the slip and retrieve the box without their knowing it, so what did they do?"

"They drugged him!" said Cortland.

"Right. Your stepmother gave him an opiate, and then Thurlow injected him with the drug that paralyzed him."

"I can see how that would keep him from going to get the box himself," said Sara. "I mean, he couldn't if he was paralyzed and couldn't move. But how was it going to help *them* get it?"

"I think I know that," said Cortland. "If he couldn't go himself, he'd have to send someone else, someone he could trust. Me."

"Right," said Wyatt. "That's why they got you down from school, thinking you'd be easy to follow when he told you where the box was. There was one complication, however. The curare, or whatever drug they injected him with, not only paralyzed him, but affected his vocal cords so he couldn't speak. While they were waiting for him to regain his voice, Andrew here found a way to communicate with him, and that was that."

"How is he?" asked Andrew. "Dr. Reeves said he thought he was better."

"He is. He's able to move and even talk a little now. It was he who told me the things I'd only guessed about his trip to Germany. And," he said, turning to Cortland, "he also told me some other things he'll undoubtedly repeat to you when you see him. For instance, how very proud of you he is for the way you've acted all through this affair."

"Oh," said Cortland, flushing with pleasure. "I'm glad that he's better and that he does think I've acted well. I've always been very fond of him and . . . Well, he's all that I've got in the way of a family now."

"When did you begin to suspect Dixon?" asked Andrew. "Did that second visit to the Admiralty have anything to do with it?"

"Yes, it did. There was something about him, his attitude toward Sir Arthur, that made me a little uneasy. Then, the morning after we got Mr. Cortland to the hospital, I received a note from him saying that Sir Arthur had asked him to get a report on Mr. Cortland's condition, find out if there had been any change. Actually, Sir Arthur had asked Dixon to get in touch with Thurlow, find out from *him* how Mr. Cortland was doing. Why was Dixon getting in touch with me?"

"Because, once Mr. Cortland was out of the Cortland house, Dr. Thurlow didn't *know* how he was doing."

"Exactly. I had one of our men check the Admiralty, and when I knew Dixon was away, I went there with you and young Cortland. I quickly discovered that Sir Arthur didn't know that Mr. Cortland had been moved to the hospital, hadn't asked Dixon to send me that note. That meant that Dixon had done it on his own—and done it for the reason you suggested. Because Thurlow could no longer tell how Mr. Cortland was doing, and Dixon had to know, had to find out if he was able to talk yet."

"I see," said Andrew.

"What I don't understand," said Sara, "is why they did it. After all, Dixon and Thurlow are British, aren't they? And wasn't Mrs. Cortland Danish?"

"She was supposed to be, a Danish countess, they said. But I did some investigating and discovered that she was actually German. She had married Captain Cortland on the orders of the German government because they thought it was important to keep an eye on him."

"What about Thurlow and Dixon?" asked Andrew.

"Thurlow is British all right, but I discovered that he went to medical school in Germany. Someone must have approached him then, and he's probably been in Germany's pay ever since. As for Dixon, who ever knows how a really great traitor's mind works, why he is willing to betray his country?"

"It seems that there's still a great deal that I don't know and that you'll have to tell me about some other time," said Verna. "All you told me before was that you were engaged in something that was terribly important. That you wanted me out of the way for a while, but that you would be responsible for the children's safety."

"That's correct," said Wyatt. "And I did everything I could in that respect. They were watched from the time they left here until they returned here."

"Those three men in the bushes outside our house," said Andrew, "they weren't with Hodge! They were your men!"

"That's right," said Wyatt. "I didn't mind your thinking that they were with Hodge and Company because that would make you go get Dixon and bring him here. But actually, one of them followed you to make sure you were all right, and the other two followed Sara and Cortland."

"But why did you want them—my stepmother and Thurlow and Dixon—here at the theatre?" asked Cortland.

"Because while it seemed innocuous, deserted and therefore a place Dixon did not have to worry about, it's actually been a sort of command post of mine for some time, a base I've been using to try to solve another case."

"The robberies that have been taking place around here in the theatre district?" guessed Cortland.

"Yes. As you saw, Burke, the watchman, is one of my men, and I have quite a few others spread out through this area. Andrew's mother and Mr. Harrison, the theatre manager, knew about it and were quite agreeable to my using it as a base. And since I had all the men I needed available around here, I thought I'd use it for another purpose—the one we just did."

"I take it that so far you haven't been able to catch the robbers or pickpockets who have been working here?" said Cortland.

"No," said Wyatt soberly. "And I'm beginning to doubt if we ever will."

"Now, now," said Tucker, who had just entered the dressing room. "Never say die. If at first you don't succeed, try and try again."

"Well, even if you haven't gotten them yet," said Sara as Wyatt looked balefully at Tucker, "isn't what you did here tonight much more important? I mean, if I had to choose, I'd rather catch a dangerous spy than some old pickpockets."

"That's right," said Tucker. "You know what they say. You can't win them all, and what you lose on the swings, you make up on the coconut shy."

"It doesn't happen to be an 'either–or' situation," said Wyatt. "I was *assigned* the job of finding the pickpockets here, and I came on this other matter entirely by accident. Besides, if I know the Admiralty and the Foreign Office, not more than a dozen people will ever hear about Dixon's trial, while the papers will be all over us again tomorrow as a bunch of bungling incompetents because of what our French friend had to say. So don't try to stay me with flagons, comfort me with apples or cheer me up with proverbs or sayings out of Samuel Smiles," he said, his voice rising and his eyes on the large and loyal Tucker, "or I'll be the one who'll be shying coconuts at your non-compos noggin!"

14

The Swings

Verna, Sara, Cortland and Andrew waited while Wyatt talked to the constable, who would be staying on duty at the theatre, then they all left together, walking up the alley toward the Strand. Cortland, bringing up the rear with Tucker, was relieved to see that—far from being disturbed by what Wyatt had said to him—the sergeant was still chuckling over it.

"Can we take you anywhere?" asked Verna when they reached the street.

"Thank you, no," said Wyatt. "I've still a great deal to do tonight: reports to make and papers to be filled out. Where's Fred?"

She nodded to where Fred waited, standing beside the carriage farther up the street and almost opposite the Savoy.

"I'll walk you that far, if I may."

"By all means."

Things were getting very lively on the Strand. In fact, more was probably going on at that hour than at any other time of the day or night. Well-dressed men and women were leaving the theatres and walking to nearby hotels or restaurants or standing under the marquees, waiting for their carriages or for a hansom or a four-wheeler. The buskers, Alf and Liz, were putting on their final performance of the evening; Liz dancing lightly to the tune of "Paddle Your Own Canoe" that Alf was squeezing out of his accordion.

"Ever been here at this time of night before?" Sara asked Cortland.

His eyes big and round, he shook his head.

"Gay, isn't it?"

He nodded.

Over the reedy wheezing of Alf's accordion, they began to hear another kind of music, the distant blaring of brasses and the insistent thumping of a drum.

"Is that our friends?" asked Andrew.

"I think so," said Sara. She looked up at Wyatt, who had paused and was standing there, frowning. "Is something wrong?"

"Yes," he said. "But I don't know what it is." Then, shrugging, he went on again with Verna.

The music became louder, clearer, and the Samaritan band appeared out of one of the side streets and came down the Strand toward them, colorful in their uniforms, the trumpets triumphant and insistent and the plump little man twinkling as he pounded on the big brass drum. The ragged and dirty urchins who ran beside them or danced after them may not have been the same ones they had seen before, but the neat and well-dressed boy who walked alongside them certainly was.

Pedestrians and theatre-goers waiting for their carriages smiled at them and dropped coins in the tambourine of the earnest-looking woman who marched near the front; and a policeman on duty near the Savoy stopped traffic to let them go by.

When Verna and the others reached her carriage, Fred saluted Wyatt, then looked over his charges: Verna, Sara, Andrew and Cortland.

"All present and accounted for," he said. "All well at your end?"

"Yes and no," said Wyatt.

"Will you be back at the theatre again tomorrow," Verna asked as he opened the carriage door for her.

"Probably," he answered. "We'll continue to use it as a base for as long as Mr. Harrison will allow us to. But I must confess—" He broke off, clapping his hand to his forehead. "Oh, my sainted aunt! Tucker, your whistle!"

With no change of expression, the imperturbable Tucker took his whistle out of his pocket and handed it to him. Stepping out into the street, Wyatt blew three shrill blasts on it.

Immediately several uniformed policemen appeared as if by magic from side streets and store entrances. A porter, a cab driver, a street hawker and a drunken French sailor—all plainclothes men in disguise—turned to look at Wyatt and wait for further instructions. He ignored them and waved to a policeman further up the Strand, almost at Villiers Street, pointing to the Samaritan band. The policeman gaped at him. Then, when Wyatt waved again, angrily and insistently, he stepped out into the street and, puzzled though he was, raised his hand, stopping the band in the middle of a spirited rendition of "Fling Out the Banner."

"Come on, Tucker," said Wyatt, and he went running up the Strand with the sergeant, Sara, Andrew and Cortland close behind him. The policeman turned to him with relief when he arrived, and the prim lady with the tambourine frowned at him.

"Would you be good enough to tell me what this is all about?" she asked.

"I'll try," said Wyatt, lifting his hat politely. "My name's Wyatt, and I'm an inspector with the Metropolitan Police."

"Well?"

"You, of course, are with the Samaritans."

"I should think that's fairly obvious."

"Do you have any identification?"

She looked at him with astonishment. "Identification? Why on earth do I need any identification?"

"Well, you do hold meetings and collect money. I should think your organization would want you to carry some sort of document to prove that you're legitimate."

"I never heard such nonsense in all my life!" she said, her voice rising. "I shall take this up with our commander! Legitimate? How can you possibly question who or what we are?"

Alf and Liz, the two Cockney buskers, had arrived at the scene with Tucker and the three young people. Alf had been listening intently, his sharp eyes roving. Now he stepped into the street and walked behind the jolly little fat man with the big drum, who was looking incredulously at Wyatt. Alf's move was so quick that Andrew couldn't follow it, but the little fat man's expression changed to one of fury as he cursed and clapped his hand to his pocket, but he was too late. By that time Alf had danced away from him and was holding aloft a man's gold watch, a ladies purse and a pearl necklace.

Again the scene changed as suddenly as it had when Wyatt had blown the whistle. The ragged urchins disappeared into the crowd. The neat and well-dressed boy tried to run, but Liza tripped him as neatly as Alf had tripped Andrew, kept him down with a foot on his chest. The lady with the tambourine looked around desperately, started to run also, but gave up when the policeman who had originally stopped her stepped in front of her.

"All right," said Wyatt. "Arrest them."

"All of them?" asked the policeman.

"All of them!"

"I don't understand," said Cortland. "Aren't they with the Samaritans?"

"Of course not," said Sara. "They're the gang of pick-pockets that Peter's been looking for. It was the kids, particularly little Goldilocks that Liz is standing on, who did the dipping. Then they passed what they got to the fat drummer who was their stall."

"That's it," said Alf who had joined them. "The little beggars are good. I've never seen one of them actually fan anyone, and of course no copper ever got one with the goods. But what made you tumble, Inspector?"

"I'm not sure," said Wyatt. "Though I've heard them and seen them dozens of times, something seemed wrong when I heard them a few minutes ago. It took me a little while to realize what it was. And it was the drum."

"The drum?"

"They're none of them really good musicians. The drummer—who's probably their leader—least of all. He just kept up a steady pounding with no variation in rhythm. But what struck me as odd, though I didn't realize it at the time, was that every once in a while, for no apparent reason, he'd stop."

"When one of the dips passed him something to put in his pocket!" said Andrew.

"That's it."

"Well, you've done it again," said Tucker gravely.

"It just goes to show what kind of education you need to get ahead on the force. Why, you've even got to be a musician. All right, all right," he said as Wyatt turned on him with mock ferocity. "After this you can shy all the coconuts you like at me, and I won't even try to dodge."